LIFA FRANK

FINAL JOURNEY OF MAN'S ETERNAL DAMNATION

Final Journey of Man's Eternal Damnation

Designed & Published in Nigeria by

TEBEBA Global Publishing Ltd.

ISBN: 978-978-766-412-4

PUBLISHER'S CONTACT:

www.tebeba.com

Info@tebeba.com

+2348186808323

DEDICATION

This book is dedicated to everyone, whether in light or in darkness, for there is a path for everyone.

ACKNOWLEDGEMENT

This book would not exist without the inspiration of the Master, who promises that my path shall shine ever brighter until the perfect day.

I extend my heartfelt thanks to everyone who has played a role in completing this book, whether knowingly or unknowingly, through their actions and ways of life. Many names are reserved in my heart and couldn't be mentioned here, but I thank you all deeply.

To my parents, Teddy and Loveth Okorie, and my brothers, your unwavering support and love have been instrumental in my growth.

If you are reading this book, it means that after numerous rounds of painstaking editing, it has finally made its way into the world. This would not have been possible without Tebeba Publisher. Thank you so much for your guidance and support.

CONTENTS

Chapter One

How did I remember all this? I sought to experience it again. It was like a drug that triggers the release of dopamine; making one to always seek a particular experience. In my case, I felt no dopamine rush. What I felt was curiosity.

'Breathe in, breathe out,' the nurse must have said to her. 'We are almost there. After a while, the cry of the baby would be heard.' She was right.

I kept pondering my date of birth. The month was January. However, my birth certificate read 7th while my mother presumed the date was 6th. Perhaps, circumstances surrounding my birth led to the very conflicts I face now.

So much has changed and a long time has passed. At present, I find myself questioning the reason for my existence. I am still unclear about Master's purpose for me, which I had hoped to have found by now. There were many questions that tormented my mind. My struggle to find answers gave rise to the restlessness that one who failed to find peace would feel.

Sometimes, I hated the fact that Mother had little faith in Master. He was the highest supernatural being who resided in heaven. He was not like other supernatural beings that some people worshipped, that have come to be their masters.

I was the only child of the family and there would always be the tendency for loneliness, as I grew up. Why didn't Mother try to have another child? Sometimes, I pitied her when I thought about the pain she had been through before giving birth to me. The fact that she had lost two children before me made her see me (the survivor) as a special being or a promised child.

There would be a stark difference between the love of a mother who couldn't have more than one child and the love of a mother who gave birth to many children; even if both had been tagged 'barren' initially. To the latter, all the children will be special. Yet, there might be favourites; just as Master had His favourites. Her love would reach her children in varying degrees.

I hated being shielded from a lot of things, as I grew. I felt like I was stuck in a prison of paradise. I wanted to be out in the world. However, this was not what my parents wanted. The promised child, which they believed I was, had to have everything on a platter. I kept wondering about what the premium, which they had placed on me, meant.

It is normal to expect both advantages and disadvantages, in anything. Beyond my complaints, I realised that there were benefits that came with being the only child.

I got the attention that Father had to offer but I couldn't grip it with both hands. It was like Master offering His love, which was sometimes elusive, to me. It felt confusing. I felt lonely, deep within, as I sought to force smiles.

Father gave me his love in more doses than necessary. A little hate would have gone a long way in preparing me for what to expect in the world.

I will have to carry my own cross, but not in the way Master carried his cross. He carried a cross to die for us, forgive our sins and save us. I carried a burden which was not mine, with the hope of discovering what path it would lead me to. This was a path I believed Master had made for me.

Oh, what have I done? I have neglected myself while carrying a burden which I believed was for the glory of Master. Why do I claim to look up to Master if indeed I looked up to myself?

I had given too much power to humans, over me. Master would be angry at what I was becoming. I had come to blame the troubles I had on some dark forces that I believed were against the plan Master had for me.

My faith in people began to diminish and my doubts increased. The values that guided me as I grew up started to shrink, also. Such values included the desire to do good rather than evil. I could not trust myself in certain situations.

I felt an emptiness inside of me. I tried to find things to fill it. I was in search of fulfilment.

There is a kind of pain that a person feels when he fails at a point when he expected to succeed; when he fails to hit the target he had envisioned. The question remains, 'What is to be done after one experiences these pains?' The answer is a choice; one either picks himself up or remains stuck.

The conquering of others has become man's earthly purpose. He sees himself as being in a race with other men. No one would like to be defeated. People hope that the sun will rise the next day so that they can rise to fight again for what they feel belongs to them. What belongs to them, really? Is it life that is made up of fleeting moments, happiness that is felt for a while before sadness comes or the legacies they strive to leave?

You are in the best position to decide what belongs to you.

As we wait for light, many have found a way to fight battles in the thickness of darkness. What tactics do they use? People are born in darkness, having lived for about 9 months in the womb. Some found purpose in darkness, while others found theirs in light. There's a path for everyone. Why did Master lead me into darkness rather than light?

Many seek to live in darkness, so as to conquer the world. Even in hell which I believed I was in, I felt that Master was with me as the little light in me sought to conquer the world.

I failed to fully recognise whether light or darkness was right or wrong, even though it was easy to categorise darkness as evil. This brought disturbing thoughts, as to where I should dwell, to me. I was stuck between light and darkness; hoping that Master would come down to tell me where I fully belonged. However, how could I tell if Master was light or darkness? If I ascend up into heaven, Master is there. If I make my bed in hell, He is also there.

In my desperate search to find a purpose for living, in the world of men, I ran into so many obstacles that I wished I were free from. To this search, there was neither a beginning nor an end; there would only be a continuation. It was like a relay race; I shall pass the baton to the next person.

I thought I was insignificant, even though I wasn't. The world had made me feel little and weak, in the face of adversity. Master would be angry at the weakness I had exhibited in the world. I sought freedom from the shackles of humans, as I believed it was the perfect key to unlock what I searched for in their world.

I couldn't even tell what it was that I searched for. I was overwhelmed by the endless questions which I had no answers to. I sought to be content with having no answers. However, I must still search, to my own displeasure, for few answers.

I tried to decipher what made it a great deal to be born out of darkness. Maybe it was the fact that light existed. After all, Master who created light and darkness wasn't insane. I would be stuck in conflict within myself on what to believe, as the spiral route of questions which I had followed would return me to the very beginning.

This beginning was the question of my very own purpose in the world. It entailed the path I had embarked on which seemed right but felt entirely wrong, the mistakes I made and the corrections I failed to note.

In what one will classify as bondage instead of freedom, in my desire to find answers, I hear voices endlessly in my small head! Do you hear them? I bet you can't.

I needed solitude, but it was not forthcoming in this prison called home. It was a prison that had been cleverly crafted to make me feel I was free in the world.

Mother's voice would bring me back to reality, out of my imaginary world where I created everyone to live in peace while each searched for the reason for his or her creation.

it was past noon on a Saturday. Why would she scream my name like I was the saviour of the world, just like people screamed Master's name when they are in need of something? I fumed as I ran to meet her. My thoughts tormented me for the rest of the day. They were about who I was and what I truly need in this world I found myself.

Days like this were undesirable. I acted lackadaisically for the rest of the day. I was angry with my mother because she stopped me from completing and fully enjoying my thoughts. I lived with doubts. I

was not sure if they were of my making, of Master's making or from another being. I tried to understand the human world and the meaning that comes with it; the world of the wise and that of the foolish.

I made plans which I wasn't ready to follow through with. I wouldn't know if the plans were wrong or right since I hadn't developed or attained high spiritual sensitivity. That would have given me access to Master who would guide me aright. My unbelieving heart hoped the plans were right.

I couldn't keep up with the demands or expectations I set for myself. Even if I came close, I would fill myself with anguish. This was aside the regrets of failed or unmet expectations. Should I settle for less? What would Master say? Worse still, what would the world say?

I couldn't bring myself to appreciate the little wins I had. I drew up plans without a back-up. I felt that having a back-up plan would signify lack of faith in the first plan I made. I am sure that other human beings faced this same issue.

The plans I made came crashing. Instead of moving on to a better plan, I began to find ways to fix the flaws I perceived in the initial plan. I did not want to be called a failure, so I sought to cover up my flaws. However, another flaw showed up.

I came to believe that I could never be perfect. Was any human perfect? If not, why did I desire to hide my flaws from others? I should have accepted myself; acceptance is the key to growth.

There's a limit to how far each person can go. No matter how strong you claim to be, there comes a time when you're unsure of yourself.

After I had tried endlessly to fix my problems without success, I gave up and chose to move on with my life. The thought of doing otherwise lingered, but I couldn't act on it. It dawned on me that darkness would never let go of light and light would keep holding on to darkness.

I claimed to be free and let my mind believe a lie. This was so I could be free from the restlessness and the pain I felt from being a flawed man. I was a fool for trying to trick a part of myself.

If one hasn't been tested, one won't know his limit or level of strength and weakness respectively. Some of my flaws seemed to vanish miraculously while others took shape; oozing out slowly at some point.

No matter how much you lie to yourself, you will be back to the reality you desired to escape from.

Was there such a thing as a flawless plan? I had come to believe that all my plans wouldn't yield results or turn out the way I envisioned them. What's the point of walking the face of the earth if I was bound to fail? I regretted my failures. With a faint heart, I had struggled to make sense of them.

I needed hope and a little faith. Since I had made plans without informing anyone, then I must take the blame. On second thought, the blame would go to Master who was the cause of everything.

Since He knows all things, He knew that this would happen. Why didn't He pull me back from doing something that was not going to work out in the long run? Did He love to see me fail? Did He desire to watch me scramble to fix a broken thing? Did He want me to watch and learn? Whatever it was, He has filled my mind with anguish and regrets.

I hated Master for letting me fail after I had made the effort to pull through in life. It appeared that there was no option before me now. I would say I was given a choice to learn from failure. Was it that easy to learn from failure?

I felt that all eyes were on me as I lost my footing but it wasn't so. Men neither knew nor desired to know me, for I had nothing to offer them. However, I still felt eyes were on me as the expectation of people, that I hoped to meet, weighed heavily on me. On the path to eternal damnation I shall find myself for failing to learn from the world that Master has placed me in.

Chapter Two

There was an obstacle to all my endeavour. I had no money. Even though I had passion, ambition and other things which I kept to myself, I failed. What good did they do me, then?

Was anyone fully successful? Whether the answer was a yes or a no, I found few people that would agree to play a less important role in the human world; even if they were so destined.

My desires for earthly pleasure made me to believe that being successful was so as to win the heart of men unto Master. I am sure that many humans were in my shoes.

How foolish I was, to set my thoughts on things in the world and not on those in heaven! How foolish the heart of men was, for trying to fool the wisest of them all, Master Himself! On the path of eternal damnation shall men find themselves for trying to fool their master, the wisest of them all, by desiring earthly pleasure for themselves while convincing themselves and others that this desire was for the glory of Master.

What is living, without a purpose? Was it a worthy purpose to seek to ignite or rekindle change in the hearts of people? Their hearts were places where different things are stored; a place where no human can ever have full access to. Only Master could get there, for I do not really understand myself sometimes. I want to do what is right but I don't do it. What I hate, I do; for as I toiled under the sun like most men did, I had come to believe that there was neither a real home for me nor peace in anything I did.

The human heart lacked love. Perhaps, I should desire to find love in a world other than this. This other world which I desired was the world of Master; the heavenly paradise which is located above or in a place I could not fully tell.

My mind was in endless turmoil as regards what was truly right for me. I was close to perishing for my lack of knowledge. I was tormented by nightmares for my failures and, few times, the nightmares had a positive effect on me; much to my own surprise.

I feared for myself and what I could become if I made headway in a path not meant for me. Why did I strive, then? Oh, what do I really want? What does the human heart really want? It would be destructive for me if I walked on a path which was not meant for me. On the path to eternal damnation shall men find themselves for walking on paths of purpose which were not meant for them

I was afraid to fail him; not Master but my father. He had envisioned so much for me and inculcated in me the expectations of a high target. To what end shall he expect great things from someone like me? Perhaps, he had expected that I do greater works than he had done. Oh, how the expectation man had from his fellow humans could either crush or build him!

Father could give me anything I desired, as long there was virtue in it and he could afford it. Despite the love and care Father gave me, there was something like a missing bond between us. I wondered what could bring two people together; perhaps some similarities or a common goal to pursue. I could not tell what was missing between Father and me; I had no idea.

I must tell you; I never had any real connection with my parents or any other human. I had come to view the human world as vicious and deadly. Yet, deep down, I desired more than anything to be closer to all humans and especially my parents. Neither of them understood what I tried to tell them. I knew they wouldn't, yet I tried to tell them, because I hoped they would. I blamed them for not trying hard enough to understand what I tried to tell them, but I was not speaking clearly. A fool I was, for not speaking clearly and yet expecting the hearts of men to fully understand what I tried to tell men! Oh, I had become dumb; striving so hard to tell the world so many things! Yet, the more I tried, the more they could barely hear or even understood me. Still, I blamed them for not trying hard enough to understand what I tried to tell them.

How could I tell them that my mind was failing me? How could I tell them that it gave rise to nightmares which sometimes helped me and at other times haunted me? How could I explain that my mind pointed at my failure to come to grips with the demands of being in the human world? How could I tell them that I felt undeserving of their love or of anything that life offers; or that my skills and efforts were no longer up to the minimum standards required to move higher?

They would be disappointed in me but not as much as I would be in myself. Despite my continuous struggle and desire to be among the best, I failed to meet expectation set by my parents, other people, Master and myself.

Master would have a reason for everything that happened but I felt that He never gave me a choice. I had failed to find where I truly belonged, among humans, and this made me become indifferent about them. I desired to be free from Master's grip, to focus more on myself and to be free from myself if that was possible.

How can one get rid of himself? If I got rid of myself, then who would I be? Who would I become? A fool I was for striving to be free from Master's grip, for there is nothing under the sun that

is hidden from Him. How can I hide from Someone who laid the foundation of the earth and knows everything about it?

Father was furious after I brought myself together to tell him of my failures, my problems and how I felt stuck in the world. It was said that honesty and communication are key factors in a relationship, but it wasn't so for me. I had made a mistake by opening myself to Father and, indeed, the world. He fumed and said a lot of harsh words to me. This was typical of Father who lacked knowledge in key areas and was not willing to learn.

I knew that whoever lacked wisdom should ask Master. I asked but never received. However, I will keep asking because I am always willing to learn.

It was not that I wasn't used to Father's angry outburst; it was that it felt different this time. His accumulation of resentment, regret and anger towards me was now unleashed. I wanted Mother to support me this time; not taking her husband's side. However, it did not happen. Was it ever said that the angels of heaven tried to leave Master's side, whether in times of war or peace? I think not, except when the devil who was once an angel did wage war. The angels have no choice, since Master is the wisest of them all. Whoever wasn't for Master was definitely against Him. Indeed, Father has become the wisest in our home. Mother would always seek to be by his side, in times of peace and trouble.

'I'm disappointed in you,' Mother said to me. I replied within me, 'I am disappointed in you all for falling to understand me. All you care about is your selfish desire that I fulfil your expectations of me.'

Looking back, it may have been wrong to let them know about my failures without giving them any explanation.

What if I have thrown away the chance of building a stronger relationship with my parents? I shall strive to regain that chance. Hardly can anything kill a parent's love for his or her children; same with Master's love for me. Anger may take over for a while, but love would be restored. Love has always been man's greatest weakness.

Shall I be a poor man for the rest of my life? That I doubt, as I shall work under the sun to make sure I have the fortune I desired; fortune which I knew belonged to Master. On the path to eternal damnation shall men find themselves for desiring that which belonged to Master.

I wondered what the true meaning of life is. The dreams of mankind unfold into various things: making a fortune, finding purpose, becoming successful and so on. Is that all life's dream is about? Is it a selfless service to humanity, done without expectations of anything in return? Shouldn't our dreams pay us? Even Master's selfless desire to die for mankind resulted in Him wanting our hearts in return. We all have to make a choice between giving our hearts to Him or not giving our hearts to Him.

Is there any human who does not desire riches? If one isn't rich, we have to presume that he or she is poor. Someone else may be at the same level as Father; stuck between riches and poverty. Sometimes, they have much and at other times, they have barely enough. Father had learnt the art of being content in any situation.

What do I deserve, in the world? I couldn't tell, but it was certainly not this restlessness and anguish. Welcome to the human world where the undeserving get what they shouldn't and the deserving get less or nothing! I know that the human world sometimes failed to hand over to you what you feel you truly deserve.

When a well placed person steps up to say, 'There is no such thing as good or bad in the world. What happens, happens. It might as well happen to a good or bad person,' I am forced to believe. This is because I had experienced life and come to conclude that this statement was true.

Sometimes, I felt that I deserved the best the world could offer because of my hard work and sacrifices. Despite these, the best still eluded me. We should definitely call it the way of nature. Here I was, still living among humans and desperate to make my parents and the humans proud! I was being foolish, because I was at an age where I should be striving for myself.

In truth, I desired to make Mother proud as I could sense that Father no longer cared. He wouldn't shed a tear, just to make sure he appeared strong and resilient. Is crying meant for women alone? Shouldn't men cry? We are allowed to cry sometimes; it shows we're human. Even Master cried when He was on earth.

Father was multifaceted. He would raise his shoulders and wax his fat muscles. He appeared to exude a surprising level of courage, which helped him to win the heart of Mother and earn the respect of most humans around him. However, one could sense that his nervousness and fear, whenever I got sick, was worse than Mother's. Love was man's greatest weakness, as Father's love for me resulted in a certain level of weakness that was displayed occasionally. Welcome to my home where Mother would sometimes play the role of Father and Father would refuse to play the role of Mother whenever it was required!

Mother would bid my father to stay strong, whenever it was necessary. I wondered how Father claimed to be strong when he was indeed weak. Then, it dawned on me that life had been conditioned such that men show traits of strength rather than weakness. The strength of men has been measured in terms of their responses in times of adversity rather than in times of peace and happiness. Parental love waxed stronger in the face of adversity, in my home.

I heard Father speak to my uncles and aunts whenever they visited us. Some often came to gather information, so as to verify whether they were doing better than Father or their children were doing better than me. The information given by Father confirmed both.

How could one derive joy from seeing another fail?

This revealed how vicious and deadly humans can be. The deceit was top-notch as some will mask their evil intentions with love and support. On the path to eternal damnation shall men find themselves for their deception and evil desires for others. I believe that Mother's endless intercessory prayers were what kept me alive or made me live longer, despite the evil ways in which I found myself.

Seeing how quick I was to condemn my aunts and uncles to eternal damnation, it won't be long before I condemned myself as my evil ways and the evil ways of the world were bound to catch up with me sometime.

I am thankful for Mother's prayers and some random good deeds I managed to have in my moral account, which I believed helped in keeping me alive, as I didn't deem myself worthy of the love Mother showed me. Maybe, she should have given up on me just like Father did.

While her prayers must have helped, I know I am here only because Master has deemed me worthy. He was giving me a chance to change for the better, His ways are different from those of men, so one could never fully comprehend them. No one except Master had complete control over life and death. Mother had only helped in delaying the inevitable that would one day come to be.

You must forgive me, for in my present state, I could neither tell which was more important nor explain what the difference was between being successful and finding my purpose. This was because everything in the present felt intertwined and wrapped into one.

I felt trapped, yet I knew that my desire to help the beings of the world made it paramount that I become better than them. How can I help another if I haven't helped myself?

I am surprised at how I found the clarity, inspiration and rigorous strength to write this. I must let you know that my thoughts were so intertwined and confusing that I failed to fully comprehend what I sought to write. It feels perfect that it became a journey, our final journey together in life, to either eternal damnation or heavenly paradise; with each of us complementing each other in our quest to find ourselves.

We are all connected in ways we never imagined. It was only modest that you and I partly became the source of inspiration for this book as I sought to understand myself before I could proceed to fully understand the world that I found myself in. It was a world that changed at will, just like me. With all my hard work and grit, I always fell short of truly believing that there was nothing in my entire life I couldn't do. There will be limits to everyone, to everything. For now, I shall keep searching until I found meaning in a meaningless order of the world I find myself.

Humans are vicious and deadly in their ways. I dare say that most will be condemned to eternal damnation. I am not exempted, as I had conceived evil desires to help me reach my targets, in a bid to get to the top. Yet, I failed to reach the top as many were not ready to relinquish their spots. Who would want to leave a great height he had attained? Even Master wasn't ready to relinquish His spot as the greatest. Those at the top schemed endlessly to make sure that they remained there.

Master had sent various messengers to the world, in a bid to both bring salvation and remain at the top. Yet, the message passed to the world by these messengers would sometimes not be fully received by men. This was due to limitations in various capacities which made it difficult for them to grow and learn. On the path to damnation shall men find themselves for not seeking help and opening themselves to learn from the world so as to become better.

I doubted my very existence, due to my endless shortcomings. I shied away from people and things I felt would make me better, even though I knew I could not survive in the world on my own.

I placed limitations on myself, as I felt I didn't have a way with words to work the minds of men in my favour. Sometimes, I felt they weren't smart enough to understand what I had to say.

Wasn't I on the path to eternal damnation, for not seeking the help that I needed to make myself better?

My failures in building relationship with my parents, friends and others in the world must have caused the loneliness I felt. I believed that I didn't need them to move forward in life, yet I was stuck. I had become like many who lied to themselves.

I had forced myself to believe that something wrong was right. I continued to hope in the future, despite my desire to not live in it. I hoped to make better connections with human hearts and in the growth of myself.

I had fears about the reason for my existence. My flaws troubled me at will and yet I got tired of endlessly trying to fix them

because I felt there was no solution. How can one who couldn't fix himself have the intent of fixing the world? A fool I was, not just for striving to make people in the world believe that I was their saviour, but also because I came to fool myself by thinking that I endlessly tried to fix my flaws.

I tried to understand myself, to no avail. I tried to feel better by being content with what I knew about myself rather than by desiring to discover new things about me. On the path to damnation shall men find themselves for not trying to discover new things about themselves.

In all this, the restlessness within me, which tormented me from a young age, remained. Sometimes, I could sense stars all over my eyes when I closed them. I would sit and feel emotions that made me wonder how could I feel all this. I had endlessly dreamt of being taken up to heaven, yet heaven felt so far away at the moment.

I had lied again, for I could never be content with myself and what I had. I kept desiring that which didn't belong to me. I wanted the whole world for myself and also for Mother, who I believed was worthy of it. On the path to damnation I shall find myself for desiring that which did not belong to me.

If Paul and Josephine would be given access to my mind where I imagined a world with only Mother and me, their anger would know no bounds as they considered themselves my close friends.

The human heart was bound to change at will, so I considered not one of them close enough to know some things about me. Even Master didn't tell people everything, when He lived on earth. Some key things were left for other messengers to speak about.

I also leave parts of myself for others to speak about, even though I can not say or know all of myself. Someone might know the surface of my mind, but not the deep parts of it. Only Master could tell what was in the recess of the hearts of men. How could I let men that changed at will know so much about me, what I can do and what I can't do?

There were times when I felt I knew all about myself but my mind couldn't focus on what it wanted. It failed to get a grip on anything. Sometimes, I prayed that Master would block my access to my mind. He had said that, 'As he [a man] thinks in his heart, so is he.' I tried to stay positive but one can't blame me if I failed to see the positive side in an evil world. I smiled on the outside while I rotted on the inside. If Master gave my mind and thoughts a free pass to become reality, then I must say that no one was to remain the world. This included even Mother whom I had claimed to love and for whom I desired everything good. I doubt whether I could ever know anything about myself.

I struggled to fit into the human world. I created a world in my mind; one that is free of pain, perfect and flawless. This world had characters that played their roles the way I wanted them to. I sought to find solace in a world that doesn't exist; the created has sought to become a creator. We are all connected and

it won't be long before the world in my mind, my desires, would slowly seep out into reality.

My aunt Susan (called Suzzy) was Father's only sibling and a widow, the richest in the family. She was close to Father and, at random times, tormented me with questions concerning my plans for the future. She constantly called to check up on me. She even invited me to come live with her so she could keep an eye on me.

I wasn't sure she truly cared about me. Therefore, I was reluctant to accept her offer initially. I could not really tell what the human heart wanted but I had few options at that moment. Thus, I had to go live with Aunt Suzzy. While I lived with Aunt Suzzy, I did not fully appreciate her incessant questions and attempts to make me better. Perhaps, when darkness fills the mind of a man, that man can only find darkness and no matter how much that man tries, light would always evade him. As stated earlier, I found Aunt Suzzy's efforts annoying and I desired that she no longer lived in this world. Few weeks later, Aunt Suzzy was dead. She had slept on a Friday night and did not wake up the next day.

Oh, my thoughts and desire have killed her! I believed that I killed her, because I had wished that she no longer walked the surface of the earth and now, she was dead. Maybe she died because it was her time to return home to Master. In any case, I was happy that she was no longer alive as she could no longer torment my soul like she had done.

However, I wasn't entirely happy as the pain she left behind would be too much for Miriam (her only child) and all who cared about as well as loved Aunt Suzzy. Mother called and complained about the effect of Aunt Suzzy's death on Father. He looked sad and gloomy, and hardly ate. I was sure that Father loved Aunt Suzzy more than anybody I could think of.

'What have I done?' I thought to myself. I remained in conflict with my mind on whether or not I was the reason for Aunt Suzzy's death. I lacked wisdom because I thought I had been given charge over the power of life and death, so as to determine who lived or died. I was indeed a fool to think I could decide when it was time for anyone to live or die. On the path to eternal damnation shall I find myself, for desiring evil and death for a beautiful creature like Aunt Suzzy.

There was a series of unrelated events which led to the moment I desired Aunt Suzzy's death. Humans are connected to each other; the death of Aunt Suzzy which I felt good about was having a domino effect on other things in the world. I feared what could happen to Father who was growing weak. Why was I afraid, though? After all, I had desired to be left alone in the world.

Mother told me that he was getting weak. Oh how trauma and pain could damage one's body and soul! I would yearn to be free of the pain that I felt whenever Mother told about the state of Father. I desired to be free of my mind so as not to bring other evil desires to reality.

If the world I created in my imagination can not rid me of this pain, then no one can escape reality. It always comes to haunt us. I was taken hostage by the pain and reality I sought to escape.

The happenings of the world would keep getting complicated and I must tell you that I knew nothing therein. I could neither tell what was to come nor fully explain what I've been through, so far in life. I was scared of the future, despite endless preparation to be in it and be ready for it.

Iwasconfidentthat Iwouldbefreeofpainintheworldofmenafter creatingmyfantasyworld,onlytorealisethatIwasn't.Noonecould be fully free of pain in the human world. Even Master couldn't free Himself from pain when He walked the earth; then tell me, how can I be free of pain? This journey would have been easier for me and I would have gotten used to it if only my mind never tricked me into believing something that was a lie. No man would ever be free of pain. Whether we consciously feel it, unconsciously repress it or leave it, we shall feel pain or be a cause of it (whether knowingly or unknowingly).

Chapter Four

It was said that those who died should rest in peace. Would my late aunt, a widow who now left an orphan, rest in peace? I pitied Miriam, Aunt Suzzy's daughter, as much as I pitied my father. I was terrified. I had the feeling that something serious was coming, but no matter how hard I tried, I couldn't really tell what it was.

I should be mourning, but I couldn't, despite what those around me felt. I sought to feel what they felt and to ease the pain they felt but I couldn't. I wasn't given the power to wipe away the pain and sufferings of the world, despite having desired it. Thus, I desired to become like Master and to do His works better than He would. Oh, how those created endlessly desire to be the Creator and to do the works of the Master better than Him! How could Master feel all the pain that existed in the world, especially that which was present right now in the house of late Aunt Suzzy, and yet be so numb that He couldn't ease it?

I couldn't feel the pain that came with the death of Aunt Suzzy, no matter how I tried. I decided it was better to feel only the pain caused by myself and to numb myself to the pain caused by the inhabitants of the world.

If I believed that Master has led me and brought me into darkness, shall I continue to ask the heavens questions without expecting an answer, as usual? With most beings of the world having twisted their thinking to believe they had become light, I would laugh at myself because no one is fully light, apart from Master who many desired to be like, and yet no one is fully darkness; apart from Master who few desire to be like.

Welcome to the world where some who claimed to be its light were the ones that caused pain and anguish to lesser beings in it! This made me wonder what the aim of being a form of light to the world was, if these people would act differently from what light entails.

Being at Aunt Suzzy's house at time of her death meant that I had to stick around longer so as not to raise any suspicion. It was not that I killed her but I always believed that I was the cause of misfortune to everyone around me. On the path of damnation I shall find myself, for thinking I was the cause of the problems of the world.

The human heart was selfish. It always wanted something for itself. This was just like how I always wanted something from the world and from Master without offering anything in return. I am sure that many people wanted the fortune of Aunt Suzzy. Many would believe, as well, that I was only at Aunt Suzzy's house because of her fortunes. However, I must tell you, I was at Aunt Suzzy's house because she loved me and because I was special to her. She always called me her little boy. She took me as the son she never had.

In my life so far, I have seen wicked and evil men who live long in their ways, as well as righteous and good men who die early in their ways. Will I, who had done a few good deeds, still die young like Aunt Suzzy? As always, there was no one way to how life works. The good could die early, just as the wicked could. The wicked could live long, just as the good could. So, if I desired to grow old, then I should become wicked, evil; righteous and good so as to throw Master off balance. This was because I had no idea if Master wanted me to live long or die young.

If I had thought about and desired the death of Aunt Suzzy, and she died despite her good deeds, then the good thoughts and desires of all those she had helped couldn't help to keep her alive. Thus, I must believe that we are here only because of Master's love and we can not question why some things happen. Well, no one really knew what was in the hearts of people and we can't even know what the world holds for us all.

There were many visitors at Aunt Suzzy's home. Most of them were distant family members while others were known to me. There were some that I did not know, too. All of them came to pay their condolences. I wasn't sure which of them was truly sad or truly happy. This is because Aunt Suzzy's altruistic qualities and fortunes didn't extend to everyone in the family. Some were left out in the cold without any help and the hard fact was that, people who did not receive anything from Aunt Suzzy must have been glad that she died.

Three days went by, but the loss still felt new. The pain still pierced the souls of those that truly cared about Aunt Suzzy. There was some news today; I was told that my parents would be coming to late Aunt Suzzy' house to pay their condolences. It was about an hour's drive (or maybe a little longer). That was something I expected but wasn't ready for. I wished that visitors would stop coming, so as to give my cousin some time alone to mourn her mother, but they wouldn't stop coming. With my parents having notified Miriam that they would be coming, I knew what to expect. I knew that my parents' coming meant a reliving of times past.

I had imagined that, despite the sombre state in Aunt Suzzy's house, Father would be quick to remind me of all my failings; to the hearing of others. While some people would be glad I wasn't doing well, others would show a form of pity. I could not let anyone know what had been happening to me.

Father's outburst was something I couldn't handle, despite having experienced it countless times. I felt sorry for my life as well as for those that I loved, whom I had failed. I must tell you, the realities of my life were getting to me. No matter how hard I tried to force my conscience to die, it would become more alive.

'How was this possible?' I would sometimes ask. This was possible because we are human and social creatures, with a certain desire to be connected to each other. So, you must forgive me when I said I wanted to be left alone. I lied, just like many did so as to feel good about themselves and to avoid the pain of their failings in the world.

Iwasn't better than many in the world and many in the world were not better than me. At a point, I would feel sorry for what I have become. In another instant, I would become happy. It dawned on me that I had succeeded in making Father unhappy; in turn, he also made me unhappy. He would have to pay for making me like this.

If someone were to ask how I was doing, I would become so quiet that such a person would become uneasy. The turbulence between my brain and mouth would convince me that it was better if I said nothing. My thoughts wandered, a lot.

Living with humans helped me see that many of them were misled by voices within them. Millions of fortune and lives were lost as many tried to escape the dreadful fate that must befall them in the world. It hurt me to see men meet their waterloo; to see their failures and misery. However, these would befall me if

I didn't change my ways. I tried to keep myself from dwelling on these thoughts but I couldn't. My consciousness was well alive, hurting me and reminding of my failures among humans.

Each person had his or her own opinion of what's right or wrong. Some even twisted the ideology of right and wrong, such that they believed something that will lead them to eternal damnation. Father was one of those that did wrong and called it right because it felt right to him. It was pointless to argue with a person's distorted perception of what's right or wrong; to each, his own desire.

I quickly packed up my few clothes and left secretly. Only my cousin Miriam knew about my departure because she helped me smuggle my things out of the house. It felt bad that I left her in her time of need. However, I needed saving and I couldn't save her. I couldn't even be there to support her.

Oh, I wished I had a sibling. I would sacrifice my life just to make him or her happy. This was what Miriam did, without asking questions. She was willing to do anything to make me happy. No matter how off the track I had gone, she would always support me. What a selfless thing she kept doing for me! On the path to eternal damnation shall men find themselves, for seeking to sacrifice themselves only for those they love rather than for the common good and betterment of the world they find themselves in; as Master has done.

Do you remember when I said I needed freedom? I lied. It was always with me. Imagine when a prisoner, who has tried to

escape so many times, gets caught and is sent back to his prison. It is likely that the gates will be flung open, one day, and he won't try to escape. This is because he has come to believe that he will be caught, any time he tries to escape. He has come to believe that hope was no more. Hope is cruel, especially when all that was hoped for never came to fruition.

We all are held by things we endlessly strive to escape from. Shall we give up hope? Shall we stop trying to escape, after endless failed attempts? Maybe I was the prisoner; maybe I wasn't. It could be you! I can't tell, but no matter what it takes, I can't give up. I must strive to get better and to escape from any strongholds that have held me. I travelled to places, in the hope that something might come alive inside of me. I must tell you, I grew restless in search of things that seemed elusive.

When I got out of Aunt Suzzy's place, I couldn't go back home. It was not that I didn't have a place called home, but that I failed to reach the minimum expectations placed on me by those at home. I wasn't discarded; they didn't have to tell me, but I had discarded myself.

I was not sure whose approval I sought: Master's, men's or mine. I knew that Master won't be happy with the pain I caused to humans.

I had fewer options than I realised. One of my close friends, who I had known since childhood, was Paul. His house seemed to be the most realistic place I could be. I knew he would always be ready to have me. He knew I wasn't used to having many people around me.

One could tell when someone was trying to be something he wasn't, like me trying to exhibit extrovert traits. That could work for a while, but at the end, it will be obvious that I wasn't an extrovert. Most times I sought a quiet place to war with my thoughts. Paul lived alone, unlike me who lacked the means for that, even though I desired to live apart from my parents.

I believed that Paul was smarter than me because he always found a way to pull through tough situations. I got stuck, often. Paul felt he could help everybody in whatever way he could. He must have gotten this trait from his parents.

I felt that Paul was more than a friend to me. We grew up on? the samestreetbeforeheandhisfamilyrelocated. Iwasn'tsureif Paul's parents were still in touch with my parents, as many years had passed since the relocation of the former. My coming here was a secret; no one else knew, except Miriam. She knows much about me, compared to my parents and others who knew little about me. I needed a place to lay my head, as I continued to wait and hope for the right inspiration that will spark up a part of myself. Thus, I will be able to move forward in my life rather than feel stuck.

I had come to Paul's residence to get away from all the tension around and within me. He welcomed me cheerfully when I arrived, but I could sense that something was off. Jessica, his

younger sister, was living with him. I could not tell whether she liked me or not. Her stare made me uncomfortable.

The last time I saw her was when she was a toddler. It dawned on me that men of the word desired to be toddlers, to be cared for and to be without worries. It was not that the toddler did not have worries but the worries were limited to a few things

Jessica suddenly looked at me, and I felt chills run down my spine. She did not say a word.

The insecurity and anxiety I felt in the world compelled me to categorise every being as vicious. I hated being myself. I was just like many humans who desired to become (like) others rather than themselves. I wondered if it was better for us to seek to become like Master and if Master had varied personalities. I had spent a lifetime trying to outrun myself. I wondered if the mistakes I made would be the summary of my life.

I quickly went into a room that Paul had offered me, without uttering a word to his sister. I just smiled at her, as I would do to anyone. I needed peace, since I was in her territory. It had been a long day. I slept off, thinking about Paul's sister, my parents and the connection of humans to each other.

The chirping of crickets coupled with the slight reflection of sunlight into my room announced a new day. My body was heavy with sleep and my mind was full of thoughts about another day among humans. I wondered at the cycle of going to sleep and waking up to the same reality that was on ground before I slept.

This was another day that I hoped I would not see; I struggled to accept the reality in which I found myself and the world that I lived in.

Did the world belong to humans or to Master? Master must have given the reins to men, only for men to make it theirs. It was like a landlord renting an apartment to a tenant. The landlord returned from a trip, only to see that the tenant had demolished the house, rebuilt it to his (the tenant's) taste and indicated that there was no place for the landlord! On the path to damnation shall men find themselves for coveting the world, which belonged to Master, for themselves.

Technological advancement has made human life complex yet easier. The same people Master created have begun to declare that He doesn't exist! One day, Master will return and take what belongs to Him. He will send the unworthy tenants unto the path of eternal damnation.

You must forgive me for sounding so judgemental. I will be among those being sent to damnation, for I coveted worldly fortune like many did. I wanted all the desires and pleasure that comes with being in the world of men. Many who have done wrong have tried to convince themselves that they have done right, so as to escape the path of damnation they shall find themselves. 'Where shall deception lead us? I wondered.

I reverenced people, just for personal gain. I cut off those that I had held in high esteem, for I felt that they weren't worth it. Was I wise or foolish? I couldn't tell. I could not find anyone as perfect

as Master and yet I desired humans to embody perfection. Was I perfect?

Some things elude man and man seeks those things that elude him so as to show that he is powerful. 'After all, Master has given us dominion over all things,' he reasons. Many have lost themselves, in hopes of finding those things that were elusive, with the biased knowledge they have that Master has given us dominion over all things.

I hate it when someone else tells me something I should have done. Sometimes, we feel that there's ample time to get things done. So, we delay doing some things that we ought to.

Paul was waking me. I was awake but not fully so. I was already conscious of my surroundings.

'Let's go for a walk,' he said.

'A walk?' I thought.

This was the very first time I had slept overnight in Paul's house, although I frequented there so as to become familiar with his parents rather than his siblings who couldn't come to accept me as his friend. A walk in this beautiful, well-arranged neighbourhood would be good. There were murals and sculptures of different types around. One could tell that this was a neighbourhood of the rich.

I set out with Paul. We stopped to greet some of his friends and neighbours. Gradually, I noticed that a walk which should provide many benefits for the physical and mental health was not showing any sign of these. Paul's friend were not ready to accept me into their group of wealthy people.

They must have felt that the poor should never be linked to the rich. How can they say this? Despite the fact that the rich and the poor meet together, Master is the maker of them all, On the path to damnation shall men find themselves for looking down on other people. I was neither rich nor poor. I did not display the amount of riches they expected, or required, for me to be welcome in their midst.

In my foolishness, I still desired the acceptance of men (in this case, Paul's friends). This was something I tried to stop, many times, but. I couldn't stop it. We are all social beings. Sometimes, men would take rejection to another level as they lacked the emotional maturity to handle it.

I tried to fit into the very situation I find myself, which was the world of the rich. Every time I tried to join a conversation, people became quiet. No one took interest in what I had to say, even though I could tell that I was smarter than them. Paul didn't try to help me out when it was required.

I said to myself, 'In this world you are in, you have nothing to say that will be accepted.' One who is alone is bound to be conquered easily. One needs others, to survive in the world. The struggle within my mind erupted into my decision not to trust anyone any more for my support. Even my mind had failed, countless times, to keep me together especially at a time like this. I began to lose trust in Master, who had remained invisible to me as I struggled to find an anchor for my faith. I blamed Master for my failures.

What happened with Paul's friends continued as we walked. At many places we visited, people acted like I wasn't there or I didn't exist. Like Master, I had become invisible to them yet I was always in their presence.

I kept trying to fit in. This culture was different from mine. Here I was, watching the children of the rich despise those they felt weren't like them. They were trying to crush the poor, but not me. They did not want to give me a chance but I couldn't be crushed. I would have to overcome the despising attitude I received. I felt the urge to kill them for causing pain to me, a fellow human. However, murder was a crime against Master and I would never come to terms with myself for taking another human's life.

Paul found much joy in this experience. I felt he was willing to lose me, rather than his friends, if the need arose. After all, I needed something from him and I believed he needed something from his rich friends. He was content with however they treated another human.

What a selfish world! I felt out of control. I felt controlled by Paul who, in this instance, held all the cards and made sure I played exactly to what he wanted. He had become like Master who played whatever He wanted to men.

This was a society of high-class individuals. It was not where I currently belonged but where I and many others envisioned to belong. I was placed by men at the bottom of the pecking order, and those I believed were at the top weren't ready to give those at the bottom a chance to work their way to the top. They were trying to crush me completely, to leave me without a fighting chance, to leave me out of consideration.

At this point, I truly feared for my existence in the world of men. Is this how my life shall turn out if I don't rise to the top? Shall I be crushed and wiped off the face of the earth, without anyone knowing about me?

Deep inside me, this wasn't the life that I wanted. I began to search, furiously and endlessly in my mind, for a way to escape this world I have found myself in. I must search for a world that would accept me, one where I would realise my potential. I had come to believe that I could never be accepted here.

With a tap on my back, I was brought back to reality and to the laughter of those around me; including Paul. 'He's lost,' they said. This statement brought back memories of what Father told my uncles and aunts about me. I realised I had become a laughing stock for people in the world.

'Let's go,' Paul said to me. 'Oh, these people don't know what's coming to them,' I said to myself. I did not know what was coming to them but I knew something would come. It was a world of cycles; something would always follow something.

I watched myself as though I was outside my own body. I saw people make fun of me and I felt so much pain. However, I immediately recalled that I had consciously wished another being misery and pain; without a second thought. I wished death for Aunt Suzzy! I wondered to myself, 'Is this madness? What have I become, really?'

The walk back to Paul's house was silent. Our consciences must judge us. In Paul's case, he had not being a good friend. I had been a weakling. Later on, maybe, I would pray that I get stronger. Master has neither given us the spirit of fear nor the desire to be weaklings but the spirit of power, love and a sound mind.

We entered the house in silence. We ate in silence. It felt as if we had taken a vow, to this effect. I felt as if I had instilled a certain form of fear in Paul. I could imagine the humans of the world trying to instil fear into Master, the creator and owner of the world. A fool I was, and I knew I shall fail horribly at my desire to instil fear into one whose authority I was under.

I would desire to please Paul, to make sure I remained in his good graces. It wouldn't be wise to be on the wrong side of Paul, for I lived with him and got many things from him. Many times in the past, despite being right, I would seek to please someone who had done wrong to me just to make sure I remained in his or her good graces.

Should I again please the world and displease myself, just to be accepted by them all? Here I was, doing it again, for I didn't have the power to bring things to my advantage. I hope, in time to come, the odds would be in my favour so I can propel myself upwards and be free of men. Now, I needed men to survive; so it made sense that I hid my thoughts from them so as to be accepted by them. On the path to damnation, I shall find myself, for hiding my thoughts from the world.

Unlike me that could conceal my feelings and sufferings for long, Paul was expressive. I always commended him for that and wished I could fully express myself the way he did. However, I couldn't. Everyone was unique in their own ways.

'I'm sorry,' Paul said to me.

'What's the essence of the apology?' I thought. I bore no grudge towards him but towards his friends. I will find ways to hurt them since I couldn't gain anything from them; at least, not in the present. Hardly have I seen anyone in his right mind who seeks to hurt the one that he gains something from.

I couldn't tell which I desired to discover - the best or worst part of myself - in the street where I have been humiliated. I haven't fully discovered myself and I hope to be discovered by others; tell me, was I being realistic?

Paul must have apologised because he needed to feel better; to lighten the burden of guilt. Or was it because I was under his roof and he could discard me at any time? Was he trying to prove a point? I couldn't really tell. Whatever the case, the damage had been done. I felt that the apology wasn't sincere or from the deepest part of his heart.

How is itthatsome menmadetheir desires known whilebelieving that they did a perfect job at hiding them? I could tell that Paul never desired to be humiliated as I had been. Humans will apologise, yet do again that which they apologised for. How merciful Master has continuously been to them!

I never believed in anything that could come from Master to myself and the world. I believed that all had failed me. I wondered why I said random prayers to Master for myself, and sometimes the world, if I never believed in Master. Lies upon lies!

Many would cheat and lie, just to get to the top. I wouldn't blame them. If the opportunity came, I shall lie to get to the top; to get ahead of those that laughed at me. Some people would be lucky while others won't be. Many will come crashing to the ground as their lies and cheating couldn't keep them at the top for long.

Chapter Five

After the episode with Paul's friends, I rejected the offer to walk with him 3 consecutive times. It seemed that morning walks were his ritual. I think he felt better for the rest of the day, after the walks. We all have that thing (we do) that helps us feel better. It could be: games, prayer, drinks, sex, meditation, music and so on. To each, their own desire.

2 days after this, I finally prepared myself for the morning walk. When Paul came into my room, he was surprised to see me up early and prepared to go out. In times past, I always desired to sleep in a bid to escape my problems. Who wouldn't want to escape the problems they have?

A fool I was, for desiring to escape my problems instead of facing them heads on. This was because, when I woke up, my problem was still there; waiting for me to find solutions to it.

On this day, I gladly accepted to walk with him. Paul was quite surprised at my zeal.

The hearts of men sometimes do not know when to stop, so they are not always ready for what's to come. I talked more than I would, which was unlike me. Paul was surprised; I could tell by the look on his face and his replies. I sought to make him uncomfortable, through the questions I asked. He stuttered as he struggled to give me answers.

I must tell you, I wasn't as vicious and deadly as other beings. I had gone over how today will be, all night, as I sought to become darkness to the hearts of men. It was not that I was light; it was that I wanted the human heart to be paid back for exploring my flaws and for making fun of me.

Every pain of the world was attributed to darkness, not light. This was flawed knowledge, I knew, but I didn't care. After all, sometimes there is pain associated with light. I just wanted to become darkness in the hope that I would inflict pain on those that hurt and made fun of me. I would be their king and they would be my subjects. It's unbelievable how quickly men would rise through the ranks - thanks to the power of intense focus, careful planning and preparation - to become higher than others. I desired to become, for now, a higher being; one who ruled over others.

The last stop before we went back home, the last time we went for a walk, was the first stop today as we set out. 'How the first could be the last and the last could be the first!' I wondered. This place was the home of those that laughed at me because they thought I was lost. I had met people who did not accept me, earlier in life, but they never openly laughed at me. This case was different.

Paul needed someone to have his back, owing to the fact that I had made him uncomfortable on the way here. After all, everyone needed a support system. The body won't feel complete without the eyes, the nose, the legs and many other parts. Each had a particular role to play in making the body whole.

The body might survive, without one of its parts, but it would never feel completely perfect. We need both body and mind, to feel whole and I felt Paul needed his friends to feel better, in this instance.

We got to a place where there was a gathering of less than 10 persons. Pleasantries were exchanged, I managed to shake the hands of people I had never met. I ignored those that laughed at me previously. I must tell you that their faces had already been permanently ingrained in my memory, owing to the pain they caused me. I could see the surprises on their face as I ignored them.

I found a seat and then got up at random. This was out of neither restlessness nor anxiety, but out of sheer confidence. I wanted to be in the faces of my oppressors and take up as much space, as well as presence, as I could. Their egos seemed to have taken a serious hit.

I observed that the rich feel much pain and anger when a poor person seeks to humiliate them. The rich will draw their resources together to crush that person off the face of the earth. This was a display of power over the weak.

I could tell they weren't happy with me but I cared not. This was a gathering of various types of men; each with their own knowledge and wisdom. Some were people whom I hoped to be associated with, in the future, and to learn something from. It would be good for each man to bring his own experience and knowledge together, in a bid to strengthen one another. We need each other to survive in the world, after all.

Despite this, my only desire at the moment, was to haunt them for causing me pain. I spoke and behaved without decorum; I behaved in a way opposite to how one was meant to behave in public and especially among people one didn't clearly know. There was silence within the group whenever I spoke, just like it was in times past. It was a silence that made everyone question why they were there.

Instead of setting myself against myself, like the last time we were here when I struggled to control my thoughts, I set them against themselves with the way I acted and talked. I no longer desired to be accepted by Paul's friends. Whatever emotions I evoked in their hearts, they shall live with. I hoped that they felt nothing but anger and disgust.

Remember when I said I was smart? I was indeed smart, in the human world. I had grown slowly by opening myself to various ideas, without having a defined idea of myself or of what I wanted.

On this day, I desired the dissatisfaction of some people. I was happy I made them uncomfortable. 'Shut up!' one of them said to me. I laughed out loud.

I did the opposite of whatever they wanted. The perfect gentlemen theywere, asnonelaidhandsonmeformakingthemangry. Imust tell you, the rich have values that they always live by. I was greatly amazed at their gentility. Does this perfect gentility really exist? Definitely, not in my neighbourhood where people resorted to violence over anything.

Itdawnedonmethattherichdesiredpeace, notviolence. However, they used both to their advantage, each when necessary. Violence was sometimes a means to an end; an end we didn't need at this moment. Many people who were present at this place got up and began to leave, individually or in pairs. Paul stood up with a smile, to leave. He didn't have to tell me; I followed suit while murmuring some words to the few that stayed back.

My planning all night had finally come to fruition. I had finally paid back those that hurt me in their own coin. However, it felt bad that some people not related to the cause of my pain, in the beginning, came to partake of my madness in this very day. The desire for vengeance has its own repercussions. It became a cause of concern to me; as to why people should be part of a pain they nothing about, to suffer the same fate for what someone else has done.

I shall not dwell on the results of my actions, as I was now so many things not usually associated with me. Maybe it was a mistake for me to come to pay them back. However, no one is to judge me; especially after what they had done to me.

In a bid to achieve my freedom, it appears that everyone else is now in bondage. Well, it is only Master - rather than an imperfect being like me -that will judge me. I did feel better for hurting those that did hurt me, even though there were collateral damages involved.

I was prepared for the wrath of Master, for having avenged myself. It is indeed a terrible thing to fall into His hands. I was so blinded by my satisfaction that I couldn't see the mistakes I had made. However, who in the world hasn't made a mistake or convinced himself that the wrong thing he did was right?

We looked to head straight home without making any stop. I talked all the way while Paul said nothing to me. I am sure I pissed him off. I talked to myself and laughed. I had finally succeeded in weakening those that seemed strong; now, they would be trying to regain their place. Never underestimate the hearts of humans and the length they can go to have what they think belongs to them, or to hurt those that hurt their egos. After all some men desired vengeance and forgot that it sometimes meant violence.

On the way home, Paul had stopped at a roadside shop to buy some things. I waited outside the shop for him. He brought 2 fruit juices and gave them to me. He went back inside and paid.

Then, he came out and took extra things without paying for them. I was angry with him. How could he do such a thing, despite all his claims of philanthropy? Why steal what you can afford? The rich and the poor, sometimes in a moment of madness, would steal and take what they could afford under the pretext that they saved for the future; a future that no one was sure of!

I must tell you, eternal damnation is closing in on the ungodly rich as well as on the poor; because of the vicious and evil thoughts they had towards the rich who sometimes stole from them.

I became silent at this point while Paul did the talking as we walked back home. How happy humans must be, causing pain to others for their own benefits, without thinking about what will happen in the long run!

At this point, I was sure he didn't think about the future, 'Man has got to survive' was used to justify a wrong.

'Let him that stole, steal no more but rather let him labour, working with his hands the thing which is good,that he may have to share with those in need.' These biblical words had no place in the world of men. Those that had more, sought to take from those that had less.

After all, 'to him that has more, more will be given and to him that has little, it will be taken from him the little he has.'

How could I labour under the sun in the world, if the work done was painful unto me? Men sought to rid themselves of pain, as well as suffering, and to made sure that their needs were met in a world that deemed many unworthy of its riches. Even I wasn't exempted.

I knew I needed to get things done and hope that, in the long run, I would be successful if Master permits. Master was the maker of the rich and poor. In the meantime, shall I endure the pain or seek to escape it? I shall seek to make a way out, whether good or bad, just like Paul did by taking some things without paying.

I had stolen before; I must tell you. Men will always see the wrong in something that's wrong, if they were not the one doing the wrong, and then choose to be blinded so as to see it as right if they were the ones doing it.

While I was angry with Paul for stealing, I had found happiness doing the same thing in times past. Perhaps, I would still be happy if an opportunity was offered to me to steal and escape the sufferings of the world. I realise that people will always criticise wrong when others do it. However, they would justify the same when they did it. On the path to damnation shall men find themselves for stealing.

Why would my mind tell me I needed to eat by taking food from another person who appeared to have enough?

If humans won't seek to help others, then is it right to take things by force, to steal or to lie so as to get it? Wouldn't eternal damnation befall me who stole because I needed to eat and had no money, and Paul who stole because he didn't want to pay? It was the same sin under different circumstances. We had compelled ourselves to believe that what we did was for a significant benefit; each man with his own selfish interest.

'There is no peace for the wicked,' Master would say. It wasn't long before I'll feel hungry again and realise that all was vanity upon vanity. I wanted food I could eat and never get hungry again, as well as water that I could drink and never get thirsty again. I wondered whether either was ever possible.

I felt restless and tormented. I wondered what I had become, as I'm sure Mother will be heartbroken if she knew what I had done in times past. The bitterness within me became so deadly that it broke my spirit.

Why was I troubled and why did all these thoughts arise in my mind? All my life has been my fault and I must make it right. I had come to acknowledge how life had been and yet I forgot all Master has done in times past, in preparations for this very moment.

Perhaps, Master prepared me for the pain I felt today. Was I ready? Was anyone ready for pain? It's hard to find anyone who is holy, despite the general profession people make that they are holy. Could the hearts of people be perfect and without sin?

Perhaps, we believe that Master was without sin only because the word had said so. Shall we then believe that I and Paul are without sin because I said so? That is up to the human heart to decide.

Chapter Six

I had spent 6 months without a word from home. It was as if my parents didn't care whether I lived or died. Or, did they care, and yet, repress their emotions?

During these 6 months I had been living in Paul's house, I had missed Aunt Suzzy's funeral. Just as her memory would slowly vanish from my heart and the hearts of others, memories of me will swiftly vanish from the hearts of people when I'm gone as well. Just like the wise, the fool will be forgotten. I didn't prepare myself for the regrets of what I've done. I wanted them to remain with me.

Miriam would be angry with me for missing the funeral Would she find a way to vent her frustration or would she repress her anger until she set her eyes on me? I hoped she wouldn't do the latter, as she would become a ticking bomb waiting to explode.

My heart felt broken as I did not pay my last rite to Aunt Suzzy, one who took me in and cared for me. I must have broken my cousin's heart, too.

Is there such a thing as a broken heart, though? I wondered at the functions of my heart. If it could pump blood round my body and be a place where different parts of my thoughts as well as emotions are stored, how then can I say that my heart is broken? To each, his own explanation.

Was this metaphorical or real? Could the broken heart be a broken mind? Which evoked emotions or showed signs of a broken heart, the body or the mind? I believe that I was heartbroken, owing to the heaviness I felt for breaking the heart of my cousin.

On the path to eternal damnation I shall find myself, for seeking to teach the world that which I didn't have complete knowledge about.

My cousin might look perfect, but I know she wasn't. When a body without legs comes knocking at your door, it may appear perfect until you look down.

How could my cousin cope without me? I had become not just her family member, but a close friend. On the path to eternal damnation I shall find myself for failing to show up for people that needed me. These were; Miriam, the world and my parents. I must humbly hate myself for not doing the right thing but who hasn't, I must also quickly pick myself for I needed to become a better person.

I had to question the workings of my mind and my body. The anger that I believed Miriam felt broke me, for I felt that I failed her. If I was broken for this reason, then the world of men should be broken for failing Master.

I concealed the outbursts of my pain due to the fact that I was still in Paul's house. I couldn't let them know of my pain. If my body breaks, then my mind should get strong by finding ways to feed on the good aspects of the world while hoping and waiting on the body to recuperate.

This was uncertain, as I had doubts concerning whether my mind would get stronger or my body would fully recuperate. Everyone doubts themselves or their strength, sometimes. Even Master, that once walked the earth, struggled with doubts at some point.

Did Master teach us how to overcome the doubt that sometimes arose within us? Did He teach us how to be strong, how to find happiness in a world that lacked it? It is up to you to decide whether Master left an answer or not. We must find answers, ourselves.

I must tell you, my doubts were so strong that if I ever went to war with them, they would be the destruction of me So, i let them go. I let them win for now, hoping to fight again sometime.

Most of the mistakes I made in life have been a result of my ignorance and foolishness. The fact that I had come to acknowledge my foolishness meant I wasn't entirely foolish at all, for if the dead can't bury the dead (like Master said), then the foolish can't know they're foolish in a world filled entirely with foolishness.

Since I existed in a world filled with both wise and foolish people, I can't tell if I'm fully foolish or fully wise. Nonetheless, my perceived foolishness had sought to set me thinking like a nonentity, that I felt I would never find my place in the world. I was here, owing to the foolishness of the first humans whose nonentity thinking made them prey to the serpent's deception.

People in the highest echelons of life sought to take the world away from Master. This was even though they controlled the world with temporary powers vested in them by Master, themselves or even people of the world. They desired to become Master and sometimes even greater than Him. On the path of eternal damnation shall those in the highest echelons of life find themselves, for their evil desire.

Welcome to the world where many want everything for themselves! Greed, they call it; but there is no one to blame for it, but ourselves who wanted all that the world can offer!

This was never Master's plan; of that I am sure. Men have become so vicious and evil that they stayed up late or sat up at night, not to pray for their own progress, but to plan and fill themselves with anguish on how to pull another being down.

Most beings sought to find someone or something to blame, for their misfortune in the world. People`s lack of contentment causes them to blame other beings for their misfortune and to find ways to bring those other beings down.

In the 6 months I had stayed at Paul's house, I didn't feel entirely at home. The house felt like a misplaced version of home, where I sought to do things on my own and to work out my path by myself.

I forgot that we are all connected in the world; a decision made today will have a corresponding effect (on another decision) tomorrow or another time.

My parents and my cousin would be disappointed in me, just as I was disappointed in myself. Was it wise for me to stay away from home? I hoped that something would come alive inside of me and propel me to a higher echelon in the world of men.

For now, I was like those found at the middle of the chain with an idea that could propel them to the highest or lowest of places. I am not above mistakes, and neither are you! If I made a mistake and sought to retrace my steps, shall men call me a failure, for seeking to make corrections? Would they be keen to cast me out of the list of those worthy of greatness if I found satisfaction In failure, in a bid to learn? So many opportunities were given to man to change himself for the better, and so many were wasted.

I shall find my place in the world. I had come to believe that not everyone was meant to get to the top. Everyone feels they have a purpose, but I doubt that, as some were kings and queens while others were pawns without a specific purpose in the world. Master, as well as the kings and queens, did as they desired, to the pawns. If everyone desires to lead, then who would be led?

In as much as I didn't want to lead or be led, I must choose a side or a side would be chosen for me. There would always be those at the bottom, who are being led, and those at the top, who lead. Thus, if I was a pawn, if my purpose was to remain at the bottom, shall I happily choose to remain at the bottom? Never! I shall begin to grow my thoughts and gain knowledge, by myself or through the help of my environment, so I could find ways to escape the bottom and work my way to the very top.

Doeseverythinghavealimit? Ithinkso. Duringthepast 6 months, I had tormented Paul in certain ways but he hasn't reacted. That's one thing to bear when you claim to be perfect, in a flawed world. Even Master showed His limit by sending men to eternal damnation after endless pleas for them to change their ways.

Maybe I won't say I tormented Paul for 6 months. There were peaceful times within those months. However, I sought to do whatever my mind found satisfaction in. It was not about whether it was right or wrong; the world of men had preferences as regards what is right or wrong.

One that had led thousands to death could be called a hero and another that saved thousands could be called a villain, but this depended on the person telling the story.

Paul's stories of me could be that I was either a hero or a villain; I could never tell. Here I was, playing both hero and villain, in the hope that I shall fit into everyone's stories of me. I cared not whether I did wrong or right. No one can hide himself forever. There were limits to get to, before someone or something would force your deepest and darkest self - that you endlessly sought to repress - to the surface.

Paul presented himself as a helper; a perfect being. He sought the approval of men before he could accept himself. Paul had let me stay for 6 months because he desired that I be under him. On the path to damnation I shall find myself, for thinking negatively about one that claimed to truly care about me. However, I couldn't tell what his true intentions were. I made assumptions, based on what I sensed from the world.

Master would be angry with people for calling upon Him mostly in times of need and trouble. We were made in His image, so maybe this is how it's meant to be. Maybe I came to Paul only in times of need.

I felt a little happy with myself, without the approval of people. I sought to become happy in who I was. I must have smiled to myself, saying I was happy with myself. Lies upon lies! I found no happiness within myself in my current state, but no matter what,

I shall put a smile on my face in the hope that I muster the strength to fight another day. I might need Paul's help later, but not now, as I sought to leave his home.

My friendship with Paul hasn't entirely been broken. When I'm gone, he will forget about the anguish and torment I caused him. It is a matter of time. Indeed, time heals and revels everything.

I will have to go back home, probably because of the news of Father's illness. After all, Father would accept me no matter how messed up I was, just like Master would always welcome a lost child.

There was always an underlying reason for everything man did, in the world of men. Consciously or unconsciously, our minds have sometimes tricked us into doing things that got us nowhere, without giving us a reason. I must tell you, for so long, I desired to hear from my parents and those I loved. Maybe, it was that I desired to return with something that would make them all proud of me, as I wasn't proud of myself.

How had I managed to become proud and not seek help from the world? On the other hand, how come I thought I could not make it in the world, even if help came? Where did the doubts come from?

I remained sad, knowing that you were sad at how I had gone off the path. I wanted to find my purpose before returning home, but it was to no avail. The perfect picture I had created in my imagination feels like it will never see the light of day. I knew I

haven't done what's expected, so as to make the world proud of me and bring my imagination as well as dreams, to reality.

Chapter Seven

Life was filled with things I have to do for myself. I had come to think of myself, more than of the world. Maybe if I had offered a little help to the world, the burden I felt would have been lighter. Service to humanity should have helped me feel better, for we are all connected in the world.

I have always desired to work out my path by myself. However, how can I do just that when the world is filled with people of different personalities, people whose paths intertwined with mine and who would either help build me up or break me down?

How could I tell if a particular person was here to build me up or break me down? There was always a dark trait that everyone tried to hide. No one wants to be seen as vicious and undesirable.

Some dark traits might be a source of fear to the bearer, a thing of concern to the world, a source of life or light to others and even a reason for the bearer's existence. However, we couldn't tell; as not everyone acknowledges one thing as simply good or simply bad.

Even Master, despite all His goodness, was once rejected and cast out by the world; before He rose to take His place as king and saviour of the world. Someday, the traits that were rejected could become accepted and the rejected people could rise to take their place at the higher echelons of the world.

The thought of losing Father made me seek to take my place at the top, so as to make him happy and to do the things expected of me. I thought I was strong, yet I felt weak. Thinking about Father's sickness made me brace myself for his death.

Oh, how the mind would easily dwell on the negatives, despite efforts to make it dwell on the positives! But how can I stop thinking about the negatives, such as death which was the destiny of every man? It is in death that we are born to eternal life.

Father was one that believed in the mystic workings of the world. He refused to go the hospital. Master would heal him, he said. Why do we have doctors then, I wondered? Why do people seek to upset the balance of the world? Let those who desire to be healed go to the doctors rather than wait on Master.

I believed that the knowledge of healing was passed from Master to humans. If there's a sickness that the doctors can't heal, let one that desired healing look steadfastly unto Master who makes the impossible possible.

Shall men say they would no longer trust in Master for healing, if the doctors healed every ailment that came their way? Fools they would be called, for they should trust and believe in Master for everything. On the path to eternal damnation shall men find themselves, for seeking to revere man more than Master; for it is Master who chooses to heal whomever He deems fit. The doctors only serve as instruments through which Master hands out small amounts of power, for the betterment of humanity.

Father would always say there is no such thing as a healthy person. This was something I would come to believe. The doctors were quick to call someone physically healthy. However, many of them did not put into consideration the mental, spiritual and emotional aspects of human well-being.

Is there anyone that is a fully whole being? My experience so far had made me believe that being emotionally unwell took a toll on both mental and physical well-being.

We are all connected, as humans, no matter how different many would claim to be. I was Master and Master was me, in a way. I was His child and He was my father. I hoped to be a father to another.

Everyone that walked the earth was made in the image of Master, yet Master has never changed. If there were different races in the world, what was Master`s image? Master was whoever and whatever we wanted Him to be.

I had hoped to rise to the top among men. Forgive me, if you feel I had judged the world unfairly, based on my perceptions and experiences so far. I felt that I was not safe, and neither was anyone. Neither in dying nor in living are we safe. In dying, one who is expected to march unto eternal life may find himself on the path of damnation. How could the world tell if someone marched unto eternal life or damnation? Well, our sensations and perceptions of what's right and wrong can help us come to half-baked speculations of where a person would end up. How could anyone be sure?

Forgive me again; my thoughts created a spiral in the hearts of others. I never intended to cause turmoil, as my conflict-laden mind mostly desired peace and happiness and yet it was missing.

Failure to free my mind and quickness to judge would drive me to insanity soon. I tried to worry less about my failures but it was to no avail. So, I sought to distance myself from my mind. How could I work independently of my mind? How could my body function on its own? My mind always gave rise to so many thoughts, claiming to have seen all that the evil world could show, Was my mind my biggest enemy? On the path to eternal damnation shall I find myself for claiming to have seen all the evil that the world has to offer.

People tend to wallow in their misery, seeking sympathy from others. Meanwhile, there will always be someone who has

had it worse. It felt like there was a race to show who owns the lowest spot. Perhaps Master is both the lowest and highest spots. In fact, the lowest spot could either be me or you. I lied to myself because I knew I wasn't the lowest and I haven't seen the worst in the world. There is no yardstick for measuring all the trauma and evil that happened therein, so, each will feel that his is the worst.

No matter how much I believed I was right, I would always feel wrong. I found myself in a world where I felt opposite of whatever I felt; good to bad, right to wrong and vice-versa. Here I was, in conflict with my mind, seeking an anchor for my hope that Father would live to see another day. Maybe I was human only to my loved ones, just as some of you are.

On the path of eternal damnation I shall find myself, for treating some beings better than others. I treated some in an evil way while I treated others in a peaceful way. Then, it dawned on me that I was neither fully healthy nor could I find anyone who was fully healthy in the world.

Visitors! Several came, for Father's sake. It was like there were more visitors at home whenever something evil happened than there were when good happened. I could never trust people. They came with smiles on their faces, which can not be relied upon. Others tried to mask their doubts about the survival of Father and another set was confident that he was going to be okay. Of course, some were indifferent.

Many visitors came together and prayed, delaying the inevitable occurrence called death. I banished any thoughts that Father won't live. If I claimed to worry no more about people, what made me worry about Father? Here I was, sitting in the world, and realising that some people won't see the light of a new day. What made me think that Father was one of them? It was fear, the fear of the unknown, that crushed the faith and hope that the strongest men had.

I knew that death was inevitable but it wasn't entirely the fear of Father`s death that plagued me. It was the fact that I did not meet the numerous high expectations he had of me. Also, he couldn't reap the reward of his labour over me. I was also scared of failing Master who had endless plans for me. It would bring so much pain to me if I couldn't find my true purpose in the world. On the path of damnation I shall find myself, if I failed Master and my father.

Fear was rising and one could feel it. Many connected the fear with the idea that Father would die while others remained steadfast in optimism that Father would recover.

We couldn't diagnose what was wrong with him. This would not be the case if he had agreed to go to the hospital. A stubborn man he was, no doubt, but to what end? Many cried unto Master, hoping for a miracle. Some who never believed in Master started to believe in Him with the hope that Father would recover.

Just like Master has promised to deliver us in times of trouble, He had given Father another chance to live.

Father fully recovered, His time hadn't come, so the spirits of death didn't have complete power over him. I must thank Master for saving me from sorrow, which I would have felt from the loss of Father whom was very sick and nearly died. Master had mercy on him and me as well.

It seems that men`s strength and faith increased in times of chaos, as many did all they could to find solutions in times of trouble. Also, Master's display of power as well as goodness drew many to Him.

Only one that had escaped death would appreciate the gift of life as well as the joy that comes with living. I could imagine Master's joy when He conquered death and returned temporarily to the earth before His ascension.

One could see Father's happiness at being given another chance to live. He suddenly changed towards me. He spoke respectfully, in a slow tone, to me; with his hands together and his eyes looking up. I felt that Father was truly grateful to Master. Our experiences in life tend to change us.

I hated him the more, now that he had fully recovered. I felt that, if he had taught me better, I wouldn't have turned out the way I did. I lacked happiness, as I lived among people; you could tell. I wanted Father to recover; now that he had recovered, I had no joy.

Of course, men are always quick to find someone or something to blame for their misfortune and misery. If only Father had become the perfect teacher he was meant to be, to me, I would have definitely turned out perfectly.

I was poor but my family wasn't. I had ambitions and dreams which I couldn't realise. This made me remain poor, at the moment. The thought of fixing my life scared me.

Can you tell me why I was not being completely grateful unto Master for saving me from sorrow, by making Father whole again? Men are quick to forget the good that was done to them; to forget quickly what Master has done for them.

Men were not entirely sure of what they want. Their greed and ignorance made it hard for them to make decisions. I couldn't tell whether I wanted Father alive so I could be saved from sorrow or if I wanted Father dead so as to be free from his high expectations of me.

It surprised me that I couldn't let go of the hate that I had for Father, despite the fact that I loved him. I wondered what I will become if I couldn't forgive Father, just like Master has forgiven my various sins.

Of what use is Master`s love and forgiveness to me if I couldn't show the same love and forgiveness to other men in the world? It had become clear that the human heart can never be fully satisfied and comprehended.

All of a sudden, Father talked a lot about religion. He spoke about Master as if he knew much about Him, yet his understanding of Master was shallow. This was because he spoke from half-baked knowledge of philosophy and human traditions, rather than from true knowledge or understanding granted by Master.

One could sense that, despite his tailored good manners and knowledge, there was a measurement missed that made everything fail to fit in perfectly.

Oh, how man sought to draw closer to Master at the point of dying! Father must have been lucky, to be saved from death and be fully healed, in the final minute.

However, I couldn't say the same for many in the world that couldn't be saved at the point of death, even though they would have desired saving. We must say a prayer for the dead and for Father, as well.

Father had accepted Master without asking for the spirit of wisdom and revelation of Master's ways unto him. Without deep thinking and understanding of the mysteries of Master, he immediately felt he needed to pay Master back for saving his life. It was important that men become grateful and thankful, not just to Master, but to other men as well.

Father was neither a true worshipper nor an atheist. He believed in Master but was like many in the world who were stuck between being saved and being fully condemned. He knew about Master but didn't know His inner workings. This applied to his family too; we knew about Master but not His inner workings.

We rarely visited the church, as I grew up, except on rare occasions. Father would always say that one found Master in his heart. I never understood what he said. How can I find something that I have no idea about?

I was doing a task. With a little extra focus, I could get it done. All of a sudden, someone screamed my name loudly. It was Mother. 'What is my name, even?' I thought.

That is why I always avoided coming home. That scream made me lose focus. 'Oh, little boy,' she said to me, 'we're going to church.'

'Oh, why, Mother?' I said to her.

'Your father commands it,' she replied.

It was in times like this that I was convinced that one never had a choice in some situations; no matter how old one was. I was always going to be my parents' little child.

'Be fast, Son,' Mother said a few seconds later, in a low tone that radiated happiness.

I couldn't tell why Mother must make me go to church with them. She probably felt I needed saving from the world or that we needed to give thanks to Master, as a family, for Father's recovery.

She made some decisions for me, acted like I was invisible and expected me to honour the decisions she made for me. It felt like I only existed because of her, which was not entirely true as

I existed because Master wanted me to be born through Mother.

'I need to leave this home,' I thought. I put on a smile to make sure that people had no clue what was going on inside of me. I had to seek counsel from my very self, in a bid to overcome the thoughts that troubled me.

Going to the local church meant I would have to meet some old friends that I felt I was better than and other old friends that I hid from. There were people whose hearts I worked my way into, in times past, only to let my guard down to the point that they had seen a little of how vicious I was.

There were some that I had cut off, owing to their pride, as I sought to break away to save myself. After all, I was all I had. I felt smart but, at some point, my smartness was leading me to the bottom of the pack where no one could hear me. This was something I knew Master would be angry with me for. I failed to use the gifts, which He had given me, wisely.

I worked my way to the minds of those I earlier mentioned because they never accepted me. However, I wanted them to accept and desire me. I wanted to be of them; I wanted to be of the world. I was ashamed now, as I had no fortune of my own despite my good looks. I couldn't ask my parents for fortune, so I could avoid one of those long talks when they would seek to lay my failures in the world at my feet.

I lied to many because I knew that, if I told the truth about what I had done, everyone would seek to cut themselves off from me. I always made sure my words conveyed little or no meaning to the world, unless I had carefully planned my words and was sure that the people I spoke to played perfectly to the way I had envisioned. I tried not to provide further explanations to some men, for I felt they could not understand me. I felt that only higher beings would understand me, without any detailed explanation.

We arrived at church, a place many believed brought them gladness. I could sense a beautiful pair of eyes, focused on me, that made me nervous. The eyes were pale blue, the face was well moulded and the red lips shone; making her stand out from the crowd.

It was Josephine, an old-time lover of mine. She walked up to me and hugged me so tightly that I remembered the old times when I endlessly worked my way to her heart, to earn her love and to be worthy of her admiration. At some point, she had been under my control.

This was one of those ladies whose love I felt I could never deserve, due to her beauty that I believed wasn't of this world. She was one of those rare beautiful creatures that made you happy if you ever talked to them, and also caused confusion in your mind as to whether what you experience with them is real.

We were short of words as we held each other, until she finally broke the silence. 'It's been a while; welcome to church. It's good that you're back.' I was neither back nor gone, but as she said those words, it felt like I was being freed from the chains of torment that had held me, so far.

I couldn't really tell how I worked my way to the heart of Josephine. I just knew that, at some point when we were together, I had her under my control and she did mostly what I desired.

The crowd fixed their eyes on us, seeking more information. I knew that humans won't miss a chance to take a hard look at those they felt were undeserving of others. I must tell you, they had forced me - at this moment - into believing that I wasn't deserving of anyone's love because of my flaws; just like they did before. I forgot that they were full of flaws, themselves.

For much of my life, I haven't seen a being that hasn't desired or searched for something and not hoped to get that which was desired or searched for. One can't tell what people truly wanted. Are we looking in the right places? Shouldn't one be searching in Master and oneself, for things desired?

The church has been a manifestation in the physical as a place for people with endless desires to congregate. It is a place where manysearchedforanswers; forgettingentirelythatweshouldgive thanks to Master for whatever we had and despite whatever problems we faced. People were here to bug Master with their problems and not to revere Him.

Tell me, if Master knew about the problems we faced, why couldn't He help us solve them and wipe them off, without us seeking Him? Master would never be angry or tired if we brought our endless problems to Him. He wanted us to, anyway. Master loved it when we always depended on Him. It was expected that Master has His place in whatever we do in the world.

The church building had 3 columns of 7 to 10 perfectly arranged seats per row. I sat at the extreme of one row and noticed a window which reflected no colour other than white. This was not the Sistine chapel that I hoped to visit. This chapel had dull colours and poor ventilation.

As the priest preached and prayed; many worshippers were screaming and shouting. Emotions were indeed high. I believed that these contributed to the poor ventilation in the building. I tried to pray without looking awfully at them,

People kept crying and screaming. I was wondering why. Was this Master? Was the outburst caused by their experiences, the desire to take things by force (for it was written that only the violent will take over the kingdom of heaven) or their response to Master's answer to their prayers? Would Master answer in the screams and shouts? Truly, Master sees it all; He knows it all. Would Master come in whispers and a calm voice, or in screams and shouts? I wouldn't know, for knowledge eludes me.

I didn't go to church a lot, so I missed some important details about Master that others who were more frequent would have learnt. Perhaps, people who served Master must have so many problems that they couldn't think and behave right. This was probably the reason for their shouting and screaming.

Oh how foolish I was to have this thought! I knew that the spirit of Master manifested in several ways. Perhaps, the spirit in me was a quiet one while that in others was a violent and screaming one. Whichever it was, all manifestations work for the glory of Master; so I must believe.

The priest was becoming like Master, as many worshippers testified of miracles they had received. Would this moment of deliverance and healing pass me by? From where I sat, I could see Father screaming that he had received a miracle. I sighed.

I walked up to the altar where the priest laid hands on me, like Master did when He was on earth. Master laid hands on men so that they received healing and miracles of all kinds. I had returned to my seat; hoping to feel different. However, I felt worse.

The fact that what tormented me raged on, at the moment I needed it to be calm, made me question whether the priest was truly working miracles and healing.

Wait, what was it that tormented me? Demons or my mind? If it was demons, then the priest's laying on of hands should have quieted the anguish inside of me. It didn't. The anguish only got worse. I was tempted to think he was a false prophet, but this belief was challenged by the great signs and wonders spoken of by others.

Was it that it wasn't my turn today? Was this priest truly of Master or of another spiritual being?

Then, in an instance, I could tell he was like most men in the world who desired something for themselves in exchange for their acts to humanity. He desired some reward for the testimonies shared. Could I call him a charlatan? Was he a manipulator?

The great signs and wonders that he worked, just like Master, now overshadowed his demands for mammon from men. I must force myself to donate, if I had received a miracle or believed in the miracles the priest said was to come. On the path to eternal damnation the priest shall find himself, for tying our blessings to the donations he demanded.

Now, I must tell you, it was right that the reward should come to the priest for seeking to help men in the world and being an instrument of progress. However, the gifts and donations should come willingly from the people. It should not be the priest demanding it by saying that only those who donated were entitled to enjoy the blessings of Master in full.

Well, even if I wanted to make a donation, I couldn't because I couldn't afford the amount he called for. I didn't even have anything for myself. Was it that the poor won't receive their blessings because they couldn't afford a specific amount? If it was so, then I must believe it was easier for the camel to enter the heavenly paradise than it was for a rich man to. Perhaps, the poor will find it easier. Since they didn't have a chance in the world they found themselves, they should work hard to ensure that they have a higher chance to enter the heavenly paradise.

However, should the poor be cast out if they couldn't afford the amount the priest demanded? Father who claimed to have received a miracle will most likely run up to the altar to lay down our house, if the priest demanded it. I wonder where we would live, if that happened.

The signs and wonders have blinded the people's eyes and hardened their hearts, so that they could neither see with their eyes nor understand with their hearts that the priest was an instrument of progress of Master and the miracles were not entirely tied to giving out a fortune.

Perhaps, if I had received my miracle, I would be willing to lay down my life for the priest. My inability to receive any miracle at the moment made me to believe that the signs and wonders the priest worked weren't real.

Now, you know why Master's disciples were willing to lay down their lives for Him. They had seen countless miracles and had come to believe in Him. It appeared that those who felt they had not experienced any good deed of His were those who wanted Him dead.

Woe betide me if I did not believe in the priest and his preaching because I haven't received my miracles. Blessed are those that believe without seeing. Was it that I couldn't believe him because he demanded mammon? Master didn't demand any mammon when He went around doing good, during His time on earth.

Why then should the priest preach that, we should follow in Master's ways if we desired to be like Him, when the priest didn't follow this? Those who claimed to have received their miracle from the priest would even lay their life for him since he had been an instrument for their saving.

Forgive me, for I couldn't speak out my concerns about the priest. His followers may seek to kill me for having little or no faith in him. He was the one that Master has used to bless them. However, they won't lay a hand on me; for Master gave them no powers over my life.

The spirit of death, which manifested in several ways, would come in the form of the followers of the priest to take me to heavenly paradise or damnation. However, my time hadn't come yet.

I wasn't sure if the priest got his power from Master or any other source. Few people could understand the mystic workings of the world. Even if his powers came from Master, Master would not condone his demand for mammon from people before they can experience Master's love and mercy.

The service ended quite quickly. I lost interest in the words of the priest. Josephine had come back. 'Why did she come back?' I said in a low tone, so she couldn't hear. After endlessly working my way to her mind in times past and not been able to fully have her, I must come to despise her.

I felt happy meeting her before the service, as it had been a long time since I saw her beautiful face. Now, I no longer desired her. It seemed that the actions of the priest were having a ripple effect.

Whatever the case, I shall seek to repress the love I still have towards Josephine for she did interest me. She stirred up a part of myself that I felt I no longer needed; the part that loved and wanted to be loved.

I was anxious to speak to her before the service but I couldn't. In fact, I was exhausted after the service. I was moody and it reflected in the way I talked to her. I was in a haste to get away from her; to continue the lingering conflict, about what is the right belief to have, within myself.

I was quiet now, just like I had been for the most part of my life. This was so I could keep myself from having the world prey on my desperate need to fit in and be among the best. In times past, I was expressive; when it came to Josephine. Currently I tried to understand what goes on in my mind without actually switching off on her.

Of all the weapons we take into battle, there is none stronger than our mind. If one wins the battle in his or her mind, then there is a chance of winning the battle on the outside; no matter the odds placed for or against the person. Here, my mind has been my greatest enemy; as it always has.

Josephine was asking me questions from a place of love and compassion, just like Aunt Suzzy did: `Where have you been? How are you? What goes on in your life now?'

What did she want me to say to her? What was she trying to find out from me? Was it that I have become that which I claimed not to be, when we were together?

With all these questions and much to my own surprise, I began to make progress and to find some peace within myself; so as to overcome the situation I found myself in. How can a person cause me internal turmoil in the way that Josephine and the priest currently did? I must expel any form of love that I still had towards Josephine or any iota of love I expected from her.

Oblivious of Josephine's presence, I began to talk slowly to myself. Soon, she tapped me to ask if everything was fine. Immediately, I began to speak to loudly to her, 'Beyond all this so-called beauty and make-up you wear to hide who you truly are; this mask that you wear to show the world an illusion of you, do you love yourself? Do you really know yourself?'

She was shocked by my sayings. Some happenings in the life of a human might leave him so shocked, that he may not know which way to go or what to say. What was there to be surprised about, since I had succeeded in corrupting my mind to be so out of touch with reality, that I had corrupted someone else and put her into conflict with herself for having come close to me?

Josephine was a soft-hearted lady who had been rocked by huge family trauma that I doubt she could ever heal from. She felt that no one was fully deserving of her love. In times past, I had tried, endlessly, to fully love Josephine and to make her mine. After I had worked my way to her mind, she had temporarily become mine and did my bidding.

Suddenly, she changed and sought to cut ties with me. She gave me no reason whatsoever. I couldn't find closure. Yet, out of my foolishness, it dawned on me that If Josephine couldn't love me, then she didn't fully love and know herself. How can you claim to love anyone if you don't love yourself? You can not give what you don't have.

Was it that she thought she couldn't find anyone deserving of her beauty? It was unbelievable how distant we had become, seeing that we were once lovers.

I felt a sense of longing, for Josephine, fused with the frustration that I could never have her. I was running out of words to say to her as I worried that my previous statement won't have the desired effect on her. It did and yet she stood by my side; looking at me with a certain conviction of either love or hatred. We needed to say our goodbyes, if we would be free from the troubles we had stirred within ourselves.

I thought, 'If she couldn't have me, then I must torment her to make sure she couldn't have anyone else.' That was foolish, as I knew Josephine had moved on swiftly from me, in times past. Still, I sought to stir up emotions to make her feel that she hadn't moved on from me; in the hope that she will love me because I still love her.

Oh, how have I come to desire that one does not have peace because peace eludes me? Josephine turned and started walking out on me. I couldn't say a word to her, as she left. I knew I lacked respect for my fellows, so I couldn't get it for myself.

I was troubled within myself. What have I done? This wasn't me.

I doubt if Josephine could ever forgive me for the anguish I must have stirred up inside of her. She had come to receive peace and gladness from the house of Master, only to have met a vicious being like me. Now, I was hoping to get her forgiveness.

How quickly my mind turned against me, so that I felt much anguish for my actions after it had stirred anguish inside of me so that I could cause anguish to another being! I felt that men couldn't give what they don't have. If I caused anguish to Josephine, it was because it was the only thing that I could give at the moment.

On the way home with my parents, my mind felt so empty and my life so lonely. Could I truly find solace in the company of my inner self as I always did in the past, when I filled it up with hope for a beautiful future? Well, definitely not today! My empty mind quickly bounced from thoughts of Josephine, to how my unfriendliness towards those who claimed to love me was tied to my foolishness, and then to my confusion on how and whether to please the hearts of men or not.

I cried bitterly within myself but did not shed a single tear. I must laugh at myself and my foolishness for claiming to do that which I didn't do. I felt like my mind became a human outside of myself; watching me and my endless mistakes without doing anything to correct me.

I must tell you, I didn't want to hurt people; especially Josephine whom I loved. I desired to find peace in a world that peace eludes. Here I was, being entirely concerned that Josephine hates me, but she wasn't the first person to hate me. It just hurts the most when those, whose love you feel you needed, showed contempt and hate. Rather than dwell on it, I would try to find solutions by raising other aspects of myself in a bid to feel better about myself.

If man wouldn't serve Master, He would raise stones to serve Him. If I couldn't get love from the world, then I must get love from myself. I must raise other aspects of myself to bury and forget what I have done to people.

What's the world without pain and sufferings?

My endless desires, as well as the fact that I could cause pain and still feel pain, meant that I was in the world. This made me conclude that one must feel pain, cause pain and have desires; to be sure one was of the world of men.

Chapter Eight

Darknesshasalwaysbeensomethingthatpeopleassociate with fear. It is something that many in the world hide from.

Before I force myself to sleep, sometimes as a means to escape the reality I found myself, my mind would be fixed on my mistakes and on the things I had failed to achieve. It always felt like something was coming to take me to where I wouldn't find myself. I knew that, if I had a little faith in myself and showed a little gratitude in my journey, I could find and be sure of myself.

In the darkness of the night, the conflict within my mind would seek to draw another nightmare to my poor soul, if I decided to sleep. I would be terrified of sleeping. How could a man like me be terrified of that which Master has created for our benefit? We all needed sleep and rest.

Tell me; is there anyone who has no fears, among humans? I think not. I would seek, in my insomnia and restlessness at night, to read books to fill up my mind with knowledge that could help me. However, the books won't help me, for I felt that whatever a man has inside of him is what he shall bring to the reality he experiences.

Soon after, I would quickly leave the books which are of no help and move to the sitting room to watch the television. This showed a news channel which was Father's favourite. This news channel would show me the latest killings and disputes between countries, the latest weaponry to be used to kill many more in the world or other news items.

As always, in the darkness, one would get a heightened sensation of something trivial. The happenings of the world made one terrified; with any sane man questioning the very reason for his existence if it would only end in death. Maybe, it was only through wars that the world could truly find peace. Did some feed on the chaos of the world or dwell in the darkness to find their purposes?

How true is it that, the greater the suffering, the more humans will be saved? Was it meant to be so, that many lives (maybe a thousand) will be lost to save one (special) life or that one life would save many?

What would be the cost of my life? Could many lives be sacrificed for my sake, just like many children were sacrificed for Master's sake? Or, shall I be among the many lives, sacrificed for the sake of another life?

I couldn't tell, as the happenings of the world were something I couldn't fully comprehend. I would become sober as I switched off the television. I couldn't watch this, not now in the middle of the night when darkness reigned.

That which I utterly enjoyed in times past was not palatable, when I was conflicted within myself. I would go back to my room to view an unclear version of the midnight stars, and the darkness that comes with it, through my window.

I could not see clearly in the darkness so I completed the midnight stars with my imagination. Nature brought me a sense of either tranquillity or destruction.

If one stared at or was in the darkness for long, could he or she finally become one with the darkness? Could he or she become a friend to it and finally hear it speak? Was it just like being called a friend of Master, whom many believed was light? Well, being in the light with Master for so long means that some special privileges and information would be passed on to you, for men spoke as moved by Master.

I found a moment of peace in nature, looking into the darkness out of my window, until a sensation arose in my mind and in my body. This signalled that someone was staring back at me.

It was as if someone was there with me, seeking to speak with me, but I couldn't hear and see who it was; for I haven't become one with the darkness so as to see or hear clearly.

I have always sought an encounter with the mystic force of the world, but not with the darkness. I didn't know what to expect or who would speak to me. My fears and my mind have stepped up to give life to something I couldn't tell had existed.

It dawned on me that our minds would always manifest something we endlessly desire or fear. Well, what can I say, with my mind having created an imaginary and invisible body that was looking at and judging me like it was outside of me? I could not really tell what to expect from myself any longer.

Oh how fear could change a lot of things!

Slowly, I felt heaviness in my eyes. My restlessness and the fear of meeting an unknown mystic force were forcing me to sleep. The sleep that I was terrified of was now becoming a saviour; how things change in the world of men! Something I had tried to avoid was becoming a saviour to me. It would help me avoid staying awake to feel the restlessness that would have tormented me till daylight, and to avoid becoming one with the darkness.

As I lay on the bed, I pondered trying to make a world a better place. It was quite bad; different people had different realities. The world was either a good or a bad place, based on this.

My mind, for its own progress, was setting better terms so I can sleep peacefully for now and then wake up again. By then, I will

be fully focused to fight on; in a world that wanted no peace for some of its inhabitants.

With a call of my name, I was already conscious enough to know what to expect. Again, what was my name?

I knew it was daybreak. I didn't even catch enough sleep, as my eyes were still heavy. Mother was quick to wake me up earlier than normal. It was the start of a new week, and I should have been filled with gratitude to Master that I had woken up again in the world of men. However, I was filled with anguish at still being among humans. My underlying hope was to live to 100 or 200 years here. Well, If wishes were horses...

I awoke, still troubled about my future; despite all my desires to live long in it. I made endless plans for the future; despite not wanting to live in it. Perhaps, my blind desire to rise to the top among people, made me fail to recognise that a lot of things could go wrong before they could finally go right.

Perhaps, either I or other people had set the bar too high. It became hard to reach my target, and this always made me feel like a failure. On the other hand, it may be that I was blind to the fact that I was making progress. Was it better not to set any bars or expectations, so that one could be happy with whatever came?

I desired that everything went right. However, due to my past failures, my mind believes that something that feels right is wrong or will turn out badly.

I wanted a lot of good things for Mother, as I felt she was the only one I could ever lay down my life for. I wanted everything for Mother; how selfish I was! To the path of damnation shall men find themselves, for their selfish motives.

I was fully awake when Mother told me that my cousin had called her. She said that Aunt Suzzy had written that her will reading should be months after her burial. I had a surprised look.

'I don't think I will go,' I said to Mother.

'Youhaveto. Miriamspeciallyrequestedyourpresence,'shereplied.

How can I summon the courage to come face to face with Miriam whom I had failed, despite endless goodwill and care from her and her mother, Aunt Suzzy? I must be ashamed of myself for having repaid good with evil.

Mother was not having another of those arguments; one could tell by the sudden change in her look which showed none of the smiles that were on display earlier. Her smiles gave way to wrinkles and her voice got deeper.

'You must respect me, as long as you're under my roof,'she said.

This was my mother. Imagine making it to heavenly paradise, only to question Master's authority there! To eternal damnation I shall be sent immediately.

She continued, 'I believe the reading is in a few days, so prepare yourself.' She walked out in anger, banging the door as she left.

I think I was happy that she was angry. She rarely closed the door whenever she entered my room.

Oh how foolish I was, for having so much joy at causing anguish to another creature! My mind was quick to judge me for having caused anguish to Mother; especially since it was very early in the morning when the sun was yet to take back power from the moon.

It dawned on me how badly I hurt Miriam and the fact that I'll have to prepare myself to face her. Are some mistakes deserving of forgiveness? I felt troubled on every side. I was knocked down but I knew it wasn't the end of me.

How can one desire to right a lifetime of wrong with another wrong, in the hope that the wrong will become right?

I was ungrateful to Mother and all those who deserved my love. I knew that Master was likely to visit His wrath on me for that, someday .

For the rest of the day, I was tormented by thoughts of my cousin as well as the sudden need for me to summon courage to speak with her. I was like an addict who hadn't taken the regular dose of his drugs; such a person would get paranoid as he or she struggled to get a hold of his or her thoughts.

I struggled to get hold of my thoughts, just as I felt pain for not being there for Miriam in her times of need. Was my failure in the world going to exclude me from the peace and sound mind that Master promised? Was I the sole cause of all that befell me, on earth? I couldn't tell.

The fact that I kept making mistakes, while pushing those that loved me away, made me to think that I was going insane. I felt like I had nothing to offer the world. A fool I was, as I dwelt only on offering material things (which I did not have) to the world. I felt that my company and the little love I could give wasn't what humans wanted.

I couldn't really tell what men wanted but I believed that Miriam would have wanted my love and company. These were things that many in the world truly need. On the path to damnation I shall find myself, for striving to give the world what I don't have.

I have to continue living this life the best way I can. I toyed with a lot of things, much to my displeasure. I always doubted my existence and this brought about sudden doubt in the existence of other creatures. If anyone helped me, I assumed I was weak but it was beyond assumption. Truly, I felt weak.

On the path to damnation shall men find themselves, for being weak and not desiring (as well as seeking) help from other men. It was advisable for me to walk in the company of others so that, if I fall, they will lift me. However, I was alone in the world. So, there was no one to help me up.

I had an underlying hate in the help that humans gave to me. In the midst of my doubts, I had sown belief into my hopeless soul that another human like me could be my saviour. It did feel like I had a thousand chances to make it big in the world of men.

I had pleas for forgiveness within me, which I shut down because I believed I would go back into doing the same thing for which I sought forgiveness; for 'If I build again the thing I destroyed, then I shall be called {foolish and} a transgressor.' I would surely be condemned to eternal damnation, which I was terrified of.

Was it worth it if I asked my cousin for forgiveness without seeking to forgive myself? Would Master forgive me for my iniquities if I would go back to doing the same things? Would I seek forgiveness from my cousin and then return to hurting her? Would I break the promises I made to her, just like I broke my promise to her mother to be a better being?

Oh, what a flawed man I was! I was an unstable man who had developed a double mind; failing to see good in an evil world of men.

Days passed and the thought of Miriam came back occasionally to either haunt or please me. Sometimes, in the right state of mind, we get to a point where we feel we can do anything we set our mind to. I felt like that now.

I sought to face the very things that caused me anguish and to correct them, but I found nothing. My mind has found solutions to everything and this surprised me. I wondered why my mind did not do this when I needed it the most.

When I was down and needed help, my mind could never get a grip on my thoughts. It would never find ways to control them when I needed it to do so, the most. I had control of my mind only when I felt happy.

Happiness in the world was truly a special feeling. How can one claim to have experienced true happiness without experiencing sadness? It has always been said that, much will be given to him that has much and that more will be taken from him that has less.

In my case, it felt different at all times. If I was happy, I would have more happiness added. Once the happiness faded and I got sad, I had more sadness added 'Breathe in, breathe out,' I would say to myself to get a grip on my thoughts. Nothing would work in my favour if I was in the wrong state of mind. I would only have control over myself when I was happy and free from all the thoughts of my failure.

When I get tormented by my failures and I seek to get control over my thoughts, nothing would work as I was in the wrong state of mind. I would only find control over myself when I was happy and free from all the thoughts of my failure. My mind would only find solutions when it was in the right state. It never prepared to find solutions in the wrong state of mind or when things went badly.

Is it not right that we prepare for war even when we want peace and we prepare for bad when we want good?

Master will be angry with, not just me, but also other humans for trying to solve our problems without seeking Him. When people think they are Master and try to solve their problems themselves without guidance or help from Him, they only end up as prey and either go back to the same problems or land in another one.

Master has said I would do greater works than Him but I doubted this, owing to the fact that I could not do that without power to control and command like Master.

Aunt Suzzy'swillwastobereadona Friday. Fatherhadcomplained that it was too early to read it but we have to respect Aunt Suzzy's wishes. Respecting the dead was a customary thing to do. Father believed that the family should be given more time to mourn.

Mother said little. I could sense that, like me, she wasn't prepared to go for the will reading. However, we had to put up a united front even though we were breaking apart inside. Why are we trying to please people? Why are we fooling ourselves, with the desire of uniting ourselves?

There were desires and thoughts so vicious that man would seek to hide them from not just men but from Master, the omniscient being whom I half-heartedly believed and desired to be like someday. Men twisted their minds so as to hide their thoughts from themselves and acted with the hope that Master wouldn't know their desires.

A fool I was, for desiring the exact powers of Master or even more foolish are men for seeking to hide their thoughts from Master, one who knows it all!

Back in my room, as I got dressed, I planned how to behave towards people in general and towards my cousin in particular. I was perceived as reserved because of my quiet demeanour. I found it quite stressful to speak to people. I sometimes replied questions with few words or a nod.

Some people were offended by these but they could not fathom what went on inside of me. Daily, I try to fix things even if they weren't broken or wrong. What could go wrong if everything went right? I perfectly prepared the words to say to Miriam, from start to finish, like I had come to the end of my life when I have no other desires but my legacy and the remembrance of me.

Just then, I began to question my mind and why it made something out of nothing. After all, man had broken endless promise made to fellow men. I was probably going to make another set of promises and even break them. Even Master has broken endless promises made to humans. Thus, I wondered if promises carried value.

On the path to damnation I shall find myself for thinking that Master's promises have returned to Him without accomplishing what they set out to do.

'A united front' was what kept on recurring in my thoughts as we made the short trip to my late aunt's home where the will reading was to take place. There would be a few people there. Did Mother really think that our family was breaking apart? She didn't say it out loud but something was off. I felt like I was breaking my family apart; after all I was meant to be the glue keeping the family together.

Children were gifts from Master. However, I was not sure if my actions made my parents feel like I wasn't a gift to them. I failed to utilise the human resources that Master has placed in the world for my happiness and progress. I failed to notice the little things that someone said, that I should have noticed, in a bid to build relationships in the world of men.

I slept at intervals and the bumps on the road jolted me to reality numerous times. I dreamt about Miriam and the proceedings ahead as it manifested in my dream state in various ways. Oh how easily our fears and desires would be transported into our dream state!

We arrived at Aunt Suzzy's house and I sought Miriam in a haste so as to make the first move to talk to her. I needed to erase any resentment she may have had towards me; if she had any towards me.

I would have been shy on a regular day but, at this moment, I was confident; to my own surprise. I saw Miriam ahead. I looked at her with much confidence and love. I hugged her tightly and, in a sheer outburst of emotions, I started crying. I was indeed surprised. Oh, how man could achieve temporary perfection sometimes! I had planned to begin with asking for forgiveness but I struggled to fit the words into the emotional-laden moment.

All of a sudden, the estate attorney interrupted us. I was delighted as I couldn't go on any longer with the words I had rehearsed.

'We have to start,' the estate attorney said.

Well, Miriam was family. She was a soft-hearted creature who was always quick to forgive, 'You are forgiven,' she said to me.

I was not sure if the words I said seemed perfect to her. Sometimes, being present is what people really need. I needed her to know how sorry I was. One could sense my remorseful state by how quiet I had become. After all, I was here only because Miriam specifically requested that I am here.

For long, I sought to hide and avoid Miriam as I couldn't find the perfect time to make peace with the one I had hurt. I must tell you, there was no time as good as the present, when it comes to making peace with Master and many others we had hurt; in the journey of life. I realised that every moment was the right moment to act.

Oh, how mysterious the ways of Master are! I was shocked when I realised that Aunt Suzzy left me quite a fortune. If only she were alive to know what I did, she would have known I was unworthy of the huge fortune she left me or the love she endlessly tried to show me.

I wept bitterly at every occasional thought of her. I was becoming more human. I pitied Miriam who had become an orphan. Aunt Suzzy took me as her child; that was the only reason she could have left me such a fortune. In a flash, I sought to leave home; to live on my own. The fortune she had willed to me and the offer of an automatic employment in her company available to me would make that happen.

Freedom! Freedom at last! Wealth! Wealth at last!

Man, on his journey, reaches a point where he feels that he can no longer go higher but only lower; no matter how hard he tries. Here, out of the blues, I was soaring higher; all thanks to one that I had caused so much pain.

But, did I cause pain to Aunt Suzzy? My mind desired the death of one I felt caused me so much pain but I didn't kill anybody. She was dead in my world but my world is not the real world. Or, tell me, has my world become the real world?

I moved out of Father's house, much against my parents' wish. They had hoped to have me under their roof and care for me much longer but I was old enough to live apart from my parents. I was old enough to make my choice. This prompted them to seek to revoke the fortune handed to me by Aunt Suzzy. They soon found that doing so was out of their power.

This wasn't like when I escaped home, or journeyed from one place to another, in the hope that something might come alive inside of me. Now, I could do whatever I wanted and everything would come alive inside of me; bringing forth light to radiate the world like Master would have wanted. He had desired that my light will shine in the world so the world will see me and thank Him for His good works in my life.

'Fortune answers all things,' the world will say to me. Would Master be proud of me if I gave all of my fortune to the sick, the poor and the needy? Shall I sacrifice all my fortune to become the poor or the needy while waiting for the sacrifice of another to help me up so I could eat?

Oh no, I would quickly rebuke this idea. It dawned on me that the road to damnation was paved with good intentions. I shall not seek to believe any of this, for I believed that Master wanted me to have the fortune. This was in the hope that I would climb the ladder of success, to the top and into the heart of men for the glory of Him. Did I gain all this, just to give it out? Of course not.

My mindwasdistorted butthatwouldn't stopmefrommovingout of Father's house and into my own house. That would be my own corner; quite far from normal human interactions and the daily activities of men. It was a place where I would be free of the hustling and bustling demands of living in the world of men.

Freedom, I must say, must elude some men. My parents incessant demands and expectations for me to do and be better caused me to escape home at will. This was without much success, as I always found a way back to them. Not any longer; I now find myself having a house of my own. It was my corner and it came with with so much freedom that I realised that anyone without self-contentment would never be free in the human world.

Open my eyes, that they should see the beauty of the world and man! Where does this beauty lie? I could speak only for myself and not for the world. Perhaps, I could find beauty in the fortunes that I now had. What if others found it in something else?

Even though everyone wants more of every good thing, none would ever desire more of the bad things on earth. Why should they? Why should I desire to have a bad thing if I felt that I had all the good things in the world? Affliction shouldn't rise the second time, but this could not apply in a world where nothing was certain. If we aren't careful, we are bound to be eaten up again by that which has destroyed us in time past.

But, sometimes, people seek to build again that which they destroyed; in the hope of finding something different.

It was not right that evil came to me when I looked for good, and that darkness came over me when I yearned for light. I thought I would have to carve a path in the darkness, having felt that I had been there for long. I must begin to decipher my way through the endless sensation and perception I feel, in the darkness. I hoped that the darkness could finally become a light on my path, so I could finally become light to see the beauty of the world and man clearly.

For long, I sought to follow those that I believed were at the top among humans. Two wrongs don't make a right. Since I felt I was wrong, I would seek to follow one who is right and to be quickly conquered by what feels right. I felt that those who are right are those who should be, or who are, at the top among humans.

Who then should follow me if I was confused on whether I was wrong or right? Those below me, those without the amount of fortune I have now are those meant to follow me. However, once they get to the level I am now, they would either desire to go higher or fall back to where they rose from if they lacked a stronghold in the level they currently found themselves.

I would seek to go higher, to desire to be like one higher than me in the world; he or she would be a mentor to me. I did not desire to be like Master, who endlessly wanted us to be like Him.

I desired to become like another human. It wasn't easy to get to the top so I must desire to be like one at the top.

My own perfect plans had failed me so many times that I felt there was no need trying to set up plans that could propel me to the top. I had fortune now, but not of my own plans. It was something I could neither explain nor expect.

A fool I was, because despite all the knowledge I acquired so far, I was still unable to rise higher than I currently was in the world. However , as it would turn out to be, I had looked up to a being like me as my mentor or my saviour who would take me to the top; in a moment of madness.

I endlessly yearned for this person. I sought to do all that he did and acquired all the knowledge I could, from him. I never sought to do the things he couldn't do because I believed that, if he couldn't do it, I couldn't do it. I was a fool and an impostor for desiring to become like another person other than myself and for looking unto another human as my saviour. On the path of damnation I am likely to be, for not accepting myself among people, not being myself in the world and desiring to become like another in the world.

As I sought to become entirely like other persons and made one like me my mentor so I could learn how he got to the top, I sought to acquire all knowledge and ideas; in a bid to be more successful. I did what they did and did not what they did not. I sought to move swiftly on the ladder of success.

I believed I had acquired the knowledge they possessed, so the path to the top would be clearer and less hectic for me. In a flash, those whose paths I had hoped to follow to the top were nowhere to be found at the top, as they came crashing to the bottom. They were below me!

I would quickly stop, retrace my steps and come up with a plan that I felt was perfect. Was it that my eyes would only see what they desired? Were they so blinded by the desire to be successful that they couldn't see the flaws of the plan I came up with? I had developed my plans and pinned my hopes on the knowledge of another being like me. This plan only got a person to the top but could not keep him or her there. Even Master's ascension to the top was fraught with endless battles that He fought and conquered, to own His place forever.

At the top where the competition is fiercest, many would go to the extreme to make sure that their spots were reserved. This left me to ponder whether it was really worth it, to ascend and then fall back, or to ascend and fight fierce battles that I may or may not win.

I wouldn't know whether I will go to the extreme to keep my place atthetopuntil Iget there. Fornow, Iamabletostopmyselfby being temporarily contented with the fortune willed to me by Aunt Suzzy. It propelled me higher but not entirely to the top. I could not tell what would have become of me if I had hastily executed the ideas I had learnt from another human being, in a bid to get to the top. Would my journey have ended? I shall keep learning and so shall you, for If we do not learn from people, what then shall become of us?

No one was perfect, nothing was truly perfect, nothing was the most beautiful. Each person viewed beauty differently. Not everyone likes me; even Master wasn't loved by all. Everyone had his or her opinion of life. Many, I was sure, wouldn't look down on me when I had nothing because of man's desire not to forget the lowly. That was in the hope that if the lowly would rise, they could be of benefit to them. To each, his or her own selfish interest; each for himself or herself.

I didn't have it all, at the moment; even the fortune that I had now which propelled me higher, was something I did not entirely work for. Does it really matter? One kills, another works hard and a third inherits; all in a bid to get the same thing. Sometimes, the one that kills, rules over everyone. Few despise him yet some praise and desire to be like the one that kills for his own selfish reasons.

Should I desire to kill, if it would get me to the top? I am yet to see anyone that loves the bottom, or that loves to work tirelessly and endlessly like an elephant under the sun while eating like an ant.

For a while, we shall cry for the departed; for those who had been killed by men to get to the top; for those who sacrificed their life so others can get to the top. We may bear resentment and anger towards those at the top; we can cry for those who had been killed but with time, everything shall be forgotten.

There is a price for everything; our lives have price tags. Shall I believe that Master and the devil bargain over them? In the world, our lives may be bought by those at the top; whether by force or by peaceful means. When we have been bought, whether by force or peace, we can't do a thing since we have not being granted access to the top by Master.

We shall come to believe that our lives have become as pawns to those who Master or the devil has permitted to get to the top (and remain there for a while), for no one truly owns the top and no one owns the bottom. In rare occasions, one at the bottom could swiftly rise to the top and one at the top could fall. Just like the pawns, the kings and queens of the world will be forgotten.

Anything will be justified, as long as it gives you a feeling of a higher purpose, gets you through the day or gives you a chance to be assured of another meal in the evil world of men. The killers and evildoers will have a perfect reason to kill and further their evil plans; even the good will further their goodly plans and sometimes, just sometimes, it leads them to a higher purpose.

'What has the world of men become, I wondered?' Master sits at the heavenly top and watches the world. His wrath is increased and He seeks to destroy the world because of man's sins. Somehow, in between, a special kind of love comes into His heart as He gives humans another chance. Perhaps, Master will never destroy the humans He created.

If I was sure that Master would never destroy the world, I must

seek even more vanity in the hope that Master's love will save me in the end. On the path to eternal damnation I shall find myself; like most people of the world, for wasting another chance that Master has given us by continuing in the evil ways that we found ourselves.

What's life without the people you love? Why did Aunt Suzzy love me so much, despite how much I felt I didn't deserve love from humans? Maybe she didn't know how vicious I was before she left me a fortune. Was I really vicious? I wouldn't know.

She gave me not just a fortune but also a place at her company whenever I wished to start a job. After all, men were never contented; they wanted more of everything. Even I, in my recklessness, had desired the world only for Mother as I wanted no one in it. Oh, how my desires would lead me to damnation!

It was not that I entirely cared, as I wanted to be free in stretching the confines of my mind. I desired to spend my life endlessly in the satisfaction of Mother so much that I left myself out of something I should be a part of. Mother had become the baseline for my sanity, so I would avoid doing things that would make her sad if she ever heard them.

I could vividly remember her crying, because of me, in times past. She was the first person to shed a tear because of me, aside Master who had shed a tear for me before sending me into the world. After all, who wouldn't cry if their loved child was sent away?

In times past, I wanted someone to understand me and to tell me what's wrong or right with me, as I failed to fully understand myself. A fool I was, for desiring the validation of humans to confirm either what's right or wrong with me. Not any longer, though, with my fortune now moving me higher than many in the world. Thus, I stopped desiring their validation. Master would never desire our praise and worship to validate His power. He remained who He is, regardless of whatever we felt we could offer Him.

Mother would always cry at my failure to find a footing in life but I was determined to survive and rise to the top. Was it that my decision not to give up before this moment showed I was strong? Would Father still feel a certain kind of pain rather than joy for the fortune willed to me, as he believed I never worked hard for it? Well, welcome to the world of men where things happen that get you confused and shocked as to how and why they happened!

I never cared what anyone said. The fortune came to me and no one could rid me of it. At the moment, I only needed to show them I'm worthy of it.

Mother and Miriam kept persuading me to work at Aunt Suzzy's company but not Father. It seemed that he never cared but I'm sure that he concealed his intentions. Deep down, he was truly happy that his son was starting to get a footing in life. Oh tell me, why shall we keep our emotions hidden from each other? Why shall we hide the need to fill a void, a void to love or be loved? I believed that, with my fortune, I can have or buy some love in the world. There were things that I knew that my fortune could buy but I couldn't know what was perfect for me.

I had yielded to Mother and Miriam's incessant demands, to work at Aunt Suzzy's company. It was called Susan Solution Company (SSC). This organisation offered a range of services such as: management consultancy, marketing, web design and others. It was a company on the rise. I was trained swiftly, to acquire the knowledge I needed to function effectively there. Tell me, is there anything man can't learn if one draws high levels of concentration, focus and determination in learning, from within?

I must tell you, deciding to work at SSC was a result of Mother's incessant demands and not of my own making, as I pulled through against my will. Mother's love and the human tendency for nepotism have landed me in a place I knew I wasn't deserving of. This showed in my first week at SSC, when I struggled to focus and finish the tasks assigned to me.

Each man has a price at which he could be bought; I too had a price at which I could be bought. Should I seek to be blind and deaf to the sufferings of others because I had fortune now which saved me from suffering?

At present, suffering had become blurred to my sight, distorted to my hearing and blocked off to my mind because of the fortune I had. My mind wasn't ready to return to its previous sufferings, so it shall seek to block me off from the thought of giving out or running out of my fortune. 'Fortune answers to everything in the world,' men would say.

It dawned on me that I was again under the influence of another being. I had become a slave to her, to do her bidding; while vanquishing any opinions or thoughts I had of it, just to have more fortune. I sold my freewill to a being like me, rather than to Master, because I desired more fortune.

There were so many in the world who hoped to sell part of their souls for a little fortune and to sell their freewill, just to get by in the world and to avoid the sufferings that were under the sun. I questioned my own desire to be part of them. I questioned my own willingness to accept the job and the fortune given to me as salary, to shut my mouth, and to be blind as well as deaf to the sufferings of the world for my own satisfaction.

'Why are you so quiet?' Sophia had said to me. She was one of the workers at SSC.

'Why would you say that?' I replied. She had asked me this particular question several times, yet I could never fully answer this question.

People do not like to be reminded of what they are. They know what and who they are. Why remind them?

Why should anyone notice me? They had to, for I stood out from the other employees with the way I dressed and the way I acted. I'm sure they would have heard of the fortune willed to me

but wouldn't dare speak to me about it. They would know I was here not because I deserved it.

I hardly noticed people. Oh, how I lied! I noticed other people but I lacked a certain attribute that was needed to relate with them. Most times, I was unwilling to speak to anyone even if they tried speaking to me. Sometimes, I not only spoke to them but also contemplated being friends with them. This made me laugh hard at myself, either in my mind or out in the open when I'm all by myself. Anyone who saw me, by chance, would come to think of me as insane.

I was indeed going crazy by being under the influence of someone when I chose to work at SSC. The fact that I had gone out of my way to talk to other beings, which was against my very nature, made me laugh very hard. I was again trying to please people. That was man's nature; sometimes returning to old ways and seeking to build again that which had been destroyed.

I was trying to woo men to myself, not on behalf of Master. I needed it; I needed to satisfy myself; I needed the other beings to be sure I existed in the world of men. We were all social creatures but I detested social gatherings as well as meetings in the workplace; even though I always had to go, Sometimes, life does not give you a choice.

I was foolish to have lived like I needed nobody; owing to my fortune. The fact that Sophia noticed me, despite how much I kept to myself since I began work, confirmed the fact that I have secret admirers and envious ones; much to my own anger and delight. I came to realise that the beauty of the world truly lies in possession of fortune, as many sought to be my friend.

Chapter Ten

I have seen so many beautiful things in the world. Could my mind fully comprehend beauty, if all was created in the image of Master? Could anyone be called beautiful or ugly? Was Master beautiful or ugly? I couldn't tell.

To Master, humans were fearfully and wonderfully made. Each person had different levels of closeness to Him. Getting to know Master deeply was not easy. It was no longer a thing of surprise that men would seek superiority over one another, to be the one closest to Master. Such a person was called 'a man after His heart.' In reality, he stole the heart of Master all for himself.

It became clear that humans will do the same things by seeking superiority over others; desiring to steal the heart of another for himself and to be the one closest to that person.

Sophia was a beautiful lady. I couldn't look her in the eyes without flinching. I believed that, if she had met me in times past, she wouldn't desire me as much as she did now. After all, in my house which has now become my corner where I could reign freely without interruption from men, I wouldn't feel the need to desire another being in it; especially one of the opposite sex.

I had failed to realise how special females are; owing to my failure to fully comprehend beautiful things in the world. I failed to connect with them but I must tell you, I struggled to connect with anyone. However, deep down, I cared a lot about men of the world and actually desired good for the world. This manifested sometimes in my desires to sacrifice my fortune to reduce the sufferings of the world.

Again, I had lied. I had lied to myself about the fact that I had desires to sacrifice my fortune for the world. Many times, our choices were selfish, in that we did whatever we liked without considering whether the choices we make might either help or hurt others.

Consciously or unconsciously, we had sometimes desired that evil befall others when they hurt us. This should not be. Vengeance is reserved for Master but people change, even though they know this. Sometimes, in a bid to avenge themselves, people desired evil to befall others.

Well, for the most part, my evil desires tended to come to light more than the good I desired. 'How so?' one may ask. Some answers must elude humans. In a desperate search for answers, there were bound to be more questions asked than answers found.

How could I trust anyone, other than Master? I lost trust in myself in some situations I found myself in. After all, I was one of those that caused me pain; in times past.

I know that some people didn't revere Master when He was on earth until He ascended. I had also ascended in the world, owing to the fortunes that I had now. I sought to question if, in poverty, one would be assured of heavenly paradise. However, I had no answers. I couldn't tell whether the rich or poor will be assured of heavenly paradise.

I shall seek to make my ways right with Master because, in a bid to ascend, I had lusted after worldly things. This was something I knew would lead me to eternal damnation. I knew I had to be dead to the things of the world to reach heavenly paradise.

Why then did worldly desires exist? Were they to tempt us or to derail us from the path to heavenly paradise? Why can't we desire and have all the beautiful things of the world? It was a choice we had to make; whether to desire worldly things or to desire Master and His ways wholeheartedly.

If in my broken state, I had few friends, shall I accept the friendship now offered to me by many; as a result of my fortune?

Or, shall I desire to be alone? If I desired to be alone, I shall find myself on the path to damnation for seeking to walk the world alone; when Master has prepared other people to journey with me, to help or hurt me, as we are all connected in the world.

I sought to do things better than most people. I desired to do my best but it never worked out. Don't tell me I didn't put in my best. When I felt I reached my limit quickly and I had nothing left to offer, it dawned on me that it was better to work in pairs so that, if one falls or reaches his limit, the other pulls him up.

Shall one who is alone suffer endlessly without seeking help? Would Master test a person's patience before helping him or her up? I was in the world but I felt different from the rest of the world. I felt that Master walked with me, owing to His always lifting me whenever I fell.

Would everyone be rewarded for doing their best? I felt I wasn't rewarded in times past for my efforts, before Aunt Suzzy left me a fortune that made me feel I reaped something I didn't sow. Yes, you can say I wasn't deserving of the fortunes willed to me. Maybe I was worse than other men, or was I?

I began to think about myself, whether I was better or worse. Well, I think we are all even, before Master. These are all lies, for I knew that some were better or worse in the eyes of Master. Master had special ones; those that He favoured more than others and who were after His heart.

Now, I had fortune that many people wanted. Many people came around me because of it. Few truly loved me. I knew I couldn't

treat the one after my heart and the one after my fortune the same way; though it was hard to distinguish between the two.

However, can I judge people for their desires? I couldn't, even if I wanted to. I had the desire, just like them, for all the happenings of the world to be in my favour.

Let's come to Sophia, my colleague. How was I sure that she truly loved me? I did not give her the attention she desired, much to her displeasure. I couldn't trust her. It was only in love that a man would seek to displease himself so as to please another; but not me. However, because of love, Master has displeased Himself to give people many chances; while delaying the destruction of the world. Shall I, because of love, give all my fortune to Sophia whom I did not trust because she desired it?

How could I feel that I was not deserving of love? I worked so hard to have Josephine's love but it proved elusive. Sophia was offering her love to me through subtle hints but I wasn't accepting it. The pain of rejection was something I had experienced countless times but I believed that Sophia was not ready to accept rejection; especially from a being like me.

People can be overly curious, especially about something they know nothing about. Many asked questions about me and my silence, especially now that I have what they sought. My silence would be uncomfortable to some in the world. After all, before I was forced out to the world and into SSC, Mother had complained for months about the fact that I lived alone. How did my living alone make her uncomfortable? After al,l the world was big enough to make everyone comfortable in their own ways. It was indeed difficult to please people. People desired what belonged to others and what they could never have.

You will be surprised at how rejection would propel someone like Sophia to display traits opposite to those of the perfect being that I claim to have known her to be. I must protect myself by asking for help from myself, the world or even Master. Hold on, is it right to protect myself from that which feels good; to protect myself from love which is the greatest commandment of them all? Was I throwing love away by rejecting Sophia's love?

At some point, no matter how much we claim to be in love, no matter all the beauty that exists in the world that we feel we deserve, if we lack self-disciple and contentment, we are bound to never be satisfied. Each human was created to satisfy another being, to complete the other person and to make the other feel less lonely. However, people tend to fill the void of loneliness with so much activity that they fail to accept their fate of being lonely in the world. People rarely accept the situation they find themselves in, especially if it is unfavourable. They keep trying to change it, for it was right that they feel ashamed of it.

Despite my fortune, I considered myself as still trying to strike a balance; considering that I had different people all around me. These were people I wasn't ready to call friends or to ask to help fill up my loneliness. This was because, when I sought to make friends and connect with people, I was tormented within myself as I couldn't find someone perfect; owing to my restlessness.

Truly, my search for someone perfect would lead to the end of me as you can not find a perfect being in the world.

So, I did not socialise much at SSC. I wanted to avoid attention, embrace my loneliness and avoid making friends who I believed would cause problems for me. After all, the world was filled with people with different personalities and temperaments; people I wasn't ready to deal with.

Still, people kept trying to talk to me; they sought my attention and wanted to do things for me. I wondered why they sought to please and do things for me because I was still in the process of fixing my life. The change in my status made it hard for people to tell that I was still lacking in some areas. I wondered if I will ever get to fix my entire life. Shall men seek to bow to me like they did to Master? Oh, I was a fool and on the path to eternal damnation I shall find myself, for desiring the kind of glory and respect that Master had.

Iwasobligedtogreetmyboss, onlysoastofindfavourinhersight. It dawned on me that many of the employees greeted and sought to please me because of personal gain. What a cyclical life man lived!

Nepotism would be grievous to anyone who isn't gaining from it. I wasn't at this company by merit or experience. It was by a rare miracle. My salary was dependent on a being like me. That was my boss; one who can seek to lay me off if she ever wanted to, in a moment of madness, and send me back fully into my corner. I sneaked out very early in the morning, from my corner, and returned to it late at night as I didn't want the world to know much about me.

My inheritance from Aunt Suzzy could keep me from working for years However, I desired more, just like many people. Mother may have pressured me to start working at SSC but it was my desire for more that made me accept the offer. I believed that it would help me to get whatever good the world could offer.

We tend to despise some beings because they had done something that was not to our satisfaction. What's the essence of being at the top if some people won't be given access to you? Not everybody will be accepted by those at the top.

Master desired the salvation of all mankind, so no one was rejected. However, men do the opposite of what Master wants. On the path of damnation we shall find ourselves, for desiring not to do things like Master but to do things in a manner that was opposite to His.

I seek to know why it is that, the good I want to do, I do not but the wrong things keeps winning even when I desired the right things. For instance, whenever I arrived at my workplace in the right frame of mind, I would seek to acknowledge those that I felt had something to offer to me. A selfish being I was, but who isn't?

People are likely to hate you if you have something they feel you aren't deserving of. I would greet my boss and, on some occasions, she would suddenly fix her gaze on me and sigh. At other times, she would reply with an attitude that was intended to infuriate me and which sometimes made me desire to stop working at SSC.

She would never take notice of me, of my height or my handsome appearance; just like I failed to notice Sophia and others in the workplace who wanted me or wanted something from me. Now, I understood and feel how others felt when I failed to acknowledge or rejected them. I often did this out of my foolish belief that I was better than them, and that they had nothing to offer me that I didn't have or couldn't afford.

Well, I couldn't offer anything to my boss that she didn't have or couldn't afford. She was starting to look down on me. I wasn't always like this; did the fortune change me? I desired a change, only to find myself doing more of that which I sought to be free from. I know that some will come to despise me, just as I despised others.

What I went through with my boss was normal to me. It surprised me, therefore, that the thought tormented me for most of the day. I wondered why, despite my fortune, anyone wouldn't accept my friendship when I offered it. Why should anyone look down on me?

No matter how perfect you think you are, someone somewhere would hate you for no reason. It could be out of anger that you claim to be perfect and they are flawed. Could it be that, sometimes, even the perfect hate the flawed for not being perfect like themselves? I was a fool for expecting to be accepted by my boss, while at the same time, I accepted some people and rejected others. On the path to damnation I shall find myself, for expecting to receive a reaction different from that which I gave to other men.

Should one keep seeking perfection, even as it eludes them? Master would be glad if a flawed being was endlessly seeking to be perfect like Him. We should not give up, for what took one person 1 year could take another 5 years. What matters is that, at the end, we will achieve perfection or whatever it is that we seek.

Shouldn't one question or seek to understand why it should take someone 5 years to get the same thing another person got in 1 year? Well, patience was lacking among humans and, I must tell you, I had no answers. Personally, I won't desire to wait 5 years for what someone else got in 1 year.

However, do we always have a say? Who is the created to question the creator? Who are men that they should question Master? They needed answers but Master answered to no one and owed nothing to any man. If it takes someone 5 years, then that is what it is. Although, men can find reasons for their misfortunes and delays, they always wanted answers to questions they asked. They wanted to know, rather than being told to wait endlessly without any explanation.

I would like to ask my boss why she hated me, the next time I greeted her and she infuriated me. I would seek for answers rather than wait for her to give me answers at her own time. For a while, she replied in a more respectful tone rather

than with silence or grunts. I was okay with this, but not entirely satisfied. This was until a day I greeted her and she was silent. I greeted her again and she didn't reply. In a moment of anger, I screamed at her with a harsh voice.

'Do you despise me?'

This startled her as she sprang out of her seat with fear in her eyes. I had excitement running through my mind.

She screamed and ordered me to leave her office. I knew that the powerful hate to be challenged but I was happy that I had made another powerful being angry.

In this instance, it seemed right that I cause pain and anguish to one that sought to cause trouble within me. I refused to leave her office even as she ordered me to,

'No, of course not. I don't despise you,' she finally spoke in a stuttering voice that conveyed her lie. Many people tend to resort to lies so as to avoid or get out of an unpleasant situation they found themselves in.

I had arrived at work today in the wrong state of mind but the fact that my boss did not reply my greeting did set me off on the wrong foot. I was angry with myself but she would have to pay. I voiced out all my repressed anguish while trashing all the respect I had for her.

Other employees were gathering towards us and I couldn't let her become the heroine in a world that I had created. She screamed at them to get back to their work stations but they didn't listen.

it dawned on me that the boss didn't infuriate just me; she infuriated most of the workers. It showed at this point, as most of them didn't obey her command.

Was I foolish for lending my voice to a voiceless people? Was I a fool to have challenged one that played a part in putting food on my table? On the path to damnation I shall find myself if I hid myself and my voice selfishly, failing to become a mouthpiece for those that needed one.

Before then, the workers had to swallow their sufferings and be silent because they had much to lose, They sold their rights and freewill to another being, just so they could have food to eat and be assured that another day's needs would be met. This was not my case, so I spoke out.

I had impressed the employees; so many of them were willing to rally around the banner I had raised. The weak and those who were not in the good books of the boss will be sure to follow me. However, how can a battle be won if I decide to lead a troop of weak soldiers therein?

This was one of those battles that, if I won, would weaken me even more. It was better if I forfeited the battle. Regardless of this thought, I had come to confirm that many in the world did hide their voice out of fear of repercussions and what to expect.

Why would the employees think I'm a leader? Why should they call me a good person? There is none good but one, which is Master. The workers needed one to follow. They needed a voice and I offered mine; much to my own displeasure because, due to

my timidity and shyness in times past , I had hid myself from the world.

I wondered how I found the confidence to confront my boss. I realised that having fortune had lifted me higher in the world of men and given me courage to confront a powerful being.

I didn't have much to lose, for if I was sacked from the workplace, I would quickly and happily retreat fully into my corner with my fortunes still able to hold me together for a long time.However, why should I feel the need to lead the workers into a revolt? Humans and Master hated revolt, but I felt the need to lead the employees out of the hell-hole that they felt they were in and into the paradise which they had envisioned for themselves. I felt called to save them from a wicked boss and leader. Was I doing all that?

I desired to lead them to where I could and then vanish, for I was neither (like) Master who is able to save them all nor consistent in my ways. They believed in me and trusted me for their greater good.

I had channelled my repressed desire to be seen and accepted by people, twisting it into the desires of the employees. They wanted the boss out of office and an increase in pay. On the other hand, I was satisfied with my pay as it didn't add much to or remove from the fortunes I had. I had doubts about whether I could be the saviour that they had envisioned.

Men often felt the need to exploit other men's weaknesses, for their own good. Many, who were desperate, were exploited by others and I knew that, at some point, humans shall seek to exploit me if I ever became desperate and needed something from them. It became hard to find any person who helped without directly or indirectly expecting something in return.

There was nothing free, among humans. When anyone offered to help me, I had to be sure of what's in it for them. Most people were self-centred; thinking mostly about themselves and whomever they held dear.

When I start to break, then everything would start to break. I will look to the skies, to find a bit of direction on how to lead those that desired that I lead them. I would close my eyes and hope for direction to come to me, to be sent to me by Master or anyone; but it was not forthcoming.

Sometimes, the world looks for a voice; for one to follow. If only one would dare speak up, to question the very order of the world! Here I was; I could finally become a voice to the voiceless. I was ready to raise the banner and they were willing to follow.

A sense of purpose was being stirred in me, as I strived to lead a bunch of people that couldn't be sure of what they truly want. I knew that the path we were upon, at this time, was going to lead to utmost destruction. I didn't know what I wanted for myself, from this, in the long run.

I believed that, in the coming destruction, I would find something or a form of safety for myself. How possible was that? How can I stop, if this brought a kind of adrenaline rush that I never

experienced? How can I stop if something wrong feels right? Tell me, how can I stop if, in the endless possibilities that this entails, I could become more successful in terms of having more fortunes and new experiences?

I knew that failure sometimes gives rise to success and that the latter takes sheer determination to sustain. I shall expel any thought of failure from my mind. What a foolish thing to do, for I could either gain less or lose more in the situation and process I found myself.

I wouldn't want to lose, so I chose to see a glimmer of hope in whatever the workers wanted. In rare occasions, the cost of winning is so much that it feels losing would be better. After all, living on earth is a risk, as one couldn't tell what was bound to happen. No one was sure whether one shall find themselves on the path to damnation or to heavenly paradise.

I shall seek to understand the world more, to take more risks, so as to find myself on whatever path I deem fit to send me. I could not comprehend what each path entails. I could not tell what happened in the world. I could not tell what was truly ugly or beautiful, as people accepted various things for their satisfaction.

Sometimes, I questioned why I still lived, despite all I have done. Sometimes, it wasn't the feeling of purpose that I still hoped to find but the higher workings of Master that I wanted my mind to fully comprehend (which it failed to do). There are few who could fully understand the workings of Master or other mystic forces.

Each of us is either winning or losing. I can't imagine being stuck in life without being sure of which way to go; although that was my situation in times past. It is important that one keeps moving.

What if trying to lead the employees was a mistake? After all, I wasn't a leader. I didn't know if I was born to lead. Remember when I asked how I could stop when something wrong feels right.

I had a hunch that this was wrong but I saw it as an opportunity to help people. I took it without checking if the odds were for or against me. What shall I do? What if this was a lost cause?

Now that the employees had gone on strike, was it certain that their pays would be increased or that the boss would be sacked? Tell me, if the employees were laid off, what shall they gain? If I was laid off as well, I still have my fortune. However, just like the employees, I can still gain less or lose much.

The employees were hasty to support one who stood to speak against the boss, without checking what it will cost. The cost of change was sometimes huge. Yet, men were happy to pay exorbitantly; just to achieve a goal. I had hoped this cause was right, for I was terrified of what's to come.

I could barely keep up with the daily demands of my mind, not to talk of carrying the burden and meeting the demands of a group of people that needed liberation from where they are. They needed to go higher, that is why they came together for a revolt. I know that men can never be fully satisfied. In their quest to have more, they could lose everything.

I believed it was right that the employees achieve their goals. We drew up plans and acted on them with full confidence. There were no back-up plans, as such would signify a lack of strong faith in the original plan we made.

Sometimes in the world, faith was not enough to see certain things to fruition. Sometimes, one does not win against a government or an institution.

Eventually, all our plans yielded no result. They came crashing to the ground, as we were all suspended indefinitely; having nothing to show for going on strike. I pitied the employees because their losses made it nearly impossible for them to muster another push to build and to avoid being entirely defeated.

They may be willing to challenge again, to sacrifice more, but maybe not with me as their leader. I was made a king without a kingdom to settle in. I must retire fully to my corner and let them raise a new king that would again lead them to destruction that was of my making.

Sometimes, one has to accept defeat and get ready to fight again. I neither accepted defeat nor resigned myself to fighting again. Miriam has become the owner of the company. Hopefully, I would be called back while the rest of my followers would be stuck in a rut. They would regret their own choices of following someone like me and deciding to make me their leader.

Should I be blamed for the failure to achieve our goals? Some factors were out of our control. The people wanted a saviour, but one can't be a saviour if one can't save himself. Only Master could save us all. On the path to damnation we shall find ourselves, for waiting on Master to save us in all situations, while He intends that we encourage and build each other.

Many in the world, had someone who had dangled in front of them, a chance that they would fight for their cause to the very end. As a result of that, men worshipped a man like them as their king and leader. 'Desperation is likely to lead men to eternal damnation,' I said to myself.

By taking a break from something, one can gain more insight and clarity. Being back in my corner was meant to give me insight as well as clarity on how to deal with the world I find myself in and to be a better person.

I was troubled and held back by the fear of trying new things. I was stuck in my old ways; conforming to that which I knew already, perhaps the fear of failure or success. I couldn't tell which it was, as I feared how people will perceive me for leading a failed revolution and for fleeing at the point the employees needed me the most.

I struggled to find balance in the world. I felt that I needed saving. Didn't the whole world need saving from the path of damnation that most shall find themselves on?

Why was I concerned with how I was perceived? After all, I was partially stuck in a rut just like my followers were but mine was different. I had led a failed revolution; perhaps, this was why the world perceived me differently. I couldn't tell if nature wanted me to be a leader or if I nurtured myself into leadership.

Men's conclusions and opinions about me neither made me feel better nor hurt me so much that I felt worse. Their opinions, which hurt me, propelled me into putting in more effort so as to prove them wrong and to show that I was worthy of being a leader. After all, we needed to be accepted by ourselves and others. As much as I was willing to go to the extreme to save myself from the hurt I felt from leading wrongfully, there was no need for that as Master makes everything perfect in His own time.

I shall laugh at myself and then proceed to motivate myself, to pull myself out of the rut I found myself. Even though my fortune hasn't entirely come from years of my hard work and sheer planning, I should thank Master that it came to me. Now that I retired to my corner for the time being, many will air their opinions of me. I did not care about that now, unlike in times past when I was very troubled about what people thought of me and sought to please them. At present, what people thought of me could only bother me a little but I came to the conclusion that I was better than them. This conclusion will perish any thought I had of what people thought of me.

I had my fortune to pull me through, for I have never seen a poor man who rules. The opinions of those below me did not count, even though I could learn from them, if there was some truth in then. I must tell you that the weak will be crushed, and the harder they tried to bring me down to their level, the more frustration and desperation they would experience.

I think a fixed pattern of life would surely do some good to people; this was a pattern of life in which we were sure what will come next. I must stop right here, for it dawned on me that I did lead people into something I didn't entirely believe in; something I wasn't willing to follow till the end. It wasn't enough that I found myself on the path to damnation; how much more that I sought to lead others into damnation as well! Oh, I led men into deception!

New experiences would sometimes bring a certain level of serenity to the human mind but It depends on the kind of experiences. Man would never desire to experience traumatic or unhappy experiences. Why would a being live under unhappy circumstances and yet take no initiative to change or improve the situation? I wondered where I would have been by now, without Aunt Suzzy's fortune. I would have been stuck in the unhappy circumstances of life and ,feel that all my initiative to change my situation would prove futile.

Now tell me, what do you think will happen if the balance of society is always maintained? It means that the poor will remain poor and the rich will remain rich. Thus, should we accept the situations we find ourselves in; whether they are favourable or unfavourable? Many wouldn't, for many desired change. There was no satisfaction, where they were.

The rich will oppress the poor as they rule while the poor desire evil for the rich so as to bring them down in order that they pay for their actions. I always sought wisdom and understanding from Master, so as to be sure of what this life fully means, but it was not forthcoming, I failed to gather much meaning from that which I had experienced so far, in life.

I had to let go of many things, as I thought there was no understanding attached to my experiences so far. This was until I got surprised when another seemed to have found meaning

and understanding in the same thing that was meaningless to me and which I struggled to understand.

This convinced me of the fact that people have different views of an event. You could have men see different things in the same picture or give a thousand meanings to a particular picture or a particular thing. One must seek to connect with others, if he or she is to make progress in life.

I had tried to do many things on my own, which never worked. Someone else tried the exact thing and It worked. Sometimes, like now, I worked in groups so as to increase competitiveness and my chance of winning. It didn't work out, despite several brains coming together for a common good and cause.

I must wonder, 'What then shall work for me?' I must feel undeserving of the things that came to me. Despite my fortune, I wanted something I worked for and truly deserved.

Should I come to see myself as a failure because I could not do some things on my own? Should I come to believe that my desires would never come to fruition? Perhaps, I should live a life without desire if none of my desires would ever become a reality.

After all, I felt that everything I had wasn't truly mine. Most of it was given to me; I didn't work fully hard for it. I presumed that it was only the dead that had no desire, as I would desire that the world will give me everything good that I asked for, without me working for it. A fool I was, going by all my foolish desires. I was secretly disappointed, despite my fortune, as I had to compromise just to pull through in life. My fortune couldn't save me from everything.

I shall come to believe that I will take and take as much as I could, without working as the world didn't want me to work individually or in groups. I shall find myself waiting for more to be added to me. I knew that, on the path to damnation I shall find myself, for my laziness and waiting for the world to give to me rather than endlessly working for what I wanted.

I failed them! I failed those that put their trust in me. The thought was always going to find its way into my mind, no matter how hard I tried to block it out. It always came at a time when I reminisced about the few beautiful moments my mind could conjure.

Slowly, my mind began to show me the faces of all those who put their trust in me, who I failed. I didn't meet their expectations of me. I tried to fathom what would happen to those that I had led wrongly, but I couldn't. However, there could be a thousand ways a particular decision we take could pan out, for everyone involved.

I thought I could have everything life had to offer, as I retired to my corner. Could I ever have everything? My corner, so far, has been a safe haven from all the dangers lurking in the world. Ever since I was suspended from the workplace and I resigned from leading a bunch of people who have perfectly irrational plans, I spent most of my time contemplating what to do next.

I started to wonder if my father will be on the path of eternal damnation or that of heavenly paradise, as he was dead. He did radiate traits of a perfect being bound for heavenly paradise, on the outside. What about the inside? How rotten was he? Well, he could still be perfect on the inside; or so I hoped.

It was ill of me to speak of my father like this, despite the fact that he didn't show perfect love and support to me. I knew that, deep within me, he tried to show that he loved and cared for me in the best possible ways. However, he was lacking in some areas, just as many in the world who were lacking in some areas.

There were many people, like Father, who sought to hide their flaws and emotions. Did they do this to show that they are stronger or more powerful? Was there any other reason, best known to them? The world can either be for us or against us. It is wise to express various emotions because we are human.

Due to my upbringing, I had learnt not to shed a tear even at the times when it was required. This was, perhaps, owing to the fact that Father didn't fully express his emotions. I had acquired the wrong knowledge from Father. Oh how parents could influence their children in many unexpected ways!

I had been wired to believe that men shouldn't express fully their emotions, so as not to appear weak. However, I manipulated myself to cry at some instances, so as to gain favours or trigger something in the hearts of people. I did not know how to let my emotions flow naturally. Indeed, the environment in which I grew up has played a role in who I had become. If my environment

had wired me to hide my emotions, then I shall nurture myself to do better.

Why would Master save Father's life only to take it back few months later? Perhaps, my ways had killed Father. His desire for my perfection had made it appear that he didn't care about me. There were many things that could cause an ageing man like Father to suddenly die of heart failure; those were the doctor's words. They helped me confirm that I wasn't entirely the cause of Father's death. It was an irony that the same doctors he disliked, when he was alive, confirmed his death.

I think that Father had everything he wanted, in his lifetime: the love of his life (my mother), me and his little fortune. He taught me that I had to work hard to survive, so I was not surprised when he tried endlessly to revoke the fortune willed to me by Aunt Suzzy. He must have felt that I didn't work hard for it.

How could I work hard if the work done under the sun was grievous unto me? I never felt too strong but I wasn't lazy. I was hard-working in my own estimation, but not up to Father's expectations. I desire abundance for myself, just like Master promised. On the path to damnation shall the lazy find themselves.

I must question the decisions I made, which got me to this point where I feel satisfied in my corner. My corner acted as a safe haven for me. Some thoughts I had in the world were hideous. I repressed them to free me of daily anguish.

Must people go to the extreme in order to get what they want, in the world. Why was it so? Why can't things always come easily? I was sad when I had to cause anyone pain in a bid to make progress or achieve something in the world. Living among humans was a ruthless struggle for survival.

I remember when I stole so I could eat and I made myself believe that it was right. What if I had died of starvation? Would it be right that I didn't steal, that I did nothing while hoping for a miracle or for someone to come to my aid? Thus, I strove to weave an element of right into something that was utterly wrong.

Why should anyone question why I stole or why should I judge anyone that stole? After all, I got not what I desired when I worked hard. If all the skills and efforts I had put into doing something right did not prevent it from going wrong, then one must question the workings of the world. Was anyone truly deserving of anything?

I felt that I was handsome. I desired love yet it eluded me. I had people offer their love to me but it wasn't theirs that I needed. I didn't even know whose love I needed. Another person would say he worked hard and desired fortune yet fortune eluded him. A third person would say he had been good and desired good things; yet good things eluded him and only bad came to him. There has never been a balance to life. The world couldn't tell whether there was any such thing as good or bad, so evil could come to either a good or bad person.

In my journey on earth, I knew I had few friends who were really there for me. How quickly bad news spread! Ever since Father's death, old friends had felt a certain need to reconnect with me. Was it worth it? Why not let sleeping dogs lie?

Paul called me. I was uneasy when he did, for I had been an ungrateful friend. We spoke for long, reigniting memories of times past. How could I forget about him? He took me in when I was not sure what I wanted for myself. It was not that it was clear now, what I wanted. It was that I had my fortune to save me.

I had not heard from him for months, yet he thought about me at those times when he felt I needed comfort and company. I was not quick to call anyone my friend but Paul offered the most in terms of friendship. He lived a selfless life and desired to please people. A fool I was, for taking a person's kindness as an act of manipulation.

Several people offered me their condolences but few were able to elicit deep emotions in me like Paul did. After all, Paul knew how to play perfectly to people's fears and desires. Josephine and Sophia called, as well. Whenever the call came in, I stared at the phone as I began to question the intentions of the caller towards me. After all, some fed on chaos to get what they want. What did they really want? I pondered what to say, hoping to find a perfect reply. In the midst of all my thinking, the phone would stop ringing. Then, my mind would quickly shift to something else that I was thinking about, before the call came in.

Ifeltthat Icouldsurvive onmy ownwithoutthe company ofothers, especially now that I had lived in solitude. I occasionally felt the need to interact with humans, as I felt I could find rest and comfort in the opposite sex. Why should I find rest in a being like me? Master has promised that the afflicted will be comforted yet I neither felt nor found any comfort in anyone in the world.

Perhaps, it would be right if one finds comfort in me rather than if I find comfort in another. I must question my intentions towards people as well as the intentions of others towards me. There was bound to be evil, among all that was done under the sun.

There comes a time where one's mind is unlocked to have a glimpse of the mind of another. This could be by actions, sensations and perceptions. One could tell when a heart is full of evil and look in shock as its owner goes a long way in hiding his hideous desires from other beings.

I must fear that evil man but I couldn't bring myself to confront him, for he can deny or be ashamed of his desires. Who could believe that one human could see the thoughts of another? Have I become like Master who knows the thoughts of humans?

I must, again, fear men who had repressed desires. This is because, when something or someone pushes him off the edge, his repressed self will begin to manifest. This could sometimes result in destruction and pain to others.

I must fear myself, for I had repressed more desires than I showed to the world; despite my endless pleas that people show their emotions. On the path of damnation shall men find themselves, for having repressed evil thoughts and desires; thoughts and desires which were not pleasant to Master or the world. Yet, these men lived in the world; never imagining anything wrong and just enjoying the beauties that come with the world.

What was I truly looking for? Was I looking for truth while I kept telling lies? The truth was sometimes accompanied by intense pain and no human was looking for pain. I needed to hear people speak the truth about themselves to me while I lied to others about myself.

I was happy that Father was no more, so I could finally conquer the world for me and Mother without having to think about Father being entirely concerned about my well-being. Others might care about me but the fact that I cared less about them meant I wasn't worthy of anybody's love; not even Father's. I had lied to people by telling them I was sad that Father was no more.

After a while, I numbed the pain that came with losing Father. Yet, memories of Father would keep flooding back to my mind at random times. I would sense his presence and see him many times in my dream state. I will seek to hear from, as well as speak to, him but it was to no avail.

it was only in dying that one will be born to eternal life. I couldn't tell where Father was; perhaps in damnation or heavenly

paradise. I could only hope he made it to the heavenly paradise. So, I would look up to the skies at random times with a smile that I struggled to keep.

Death was a part of our existence. It was our destiny. I was quick to acknowledge these and brace myself for when death would come to take, not just me, but all of us to either damnation or heavenly paradise. For now, I lived in the world; hoping that at long last, my purpose would become clearer.

Chapter Twelve

Most times, it is when something has gone wrong that people remember others. Sometimes, men were more willing to spread bad news than they were to spread good news. The good you do will be remembered by some but few would accept it without an element of doubt. The human heart sometimes hinders the good from spreading because of human spite and selfishness, as they weren't the one that experienced the good.

Despite my fortune, some people never believed I was good. Their only memory of me was bad. I never spoke for the world; who am I to do so? To whom shall the world hand the power, to become its mouthpiece? It was better to speak for yourself and, if men follow your ways, so shall it be. I spoke for myself and never expected people to follow my ways. I expected nothing from the world, and especially not from men who sought different things in the same world. To each, his or her opinion and desire.

One dare not claim to be as powerful as to speak for the world. Even Master who lived on earth and died for humans wouldn't say He spoke for everyone as He wasn't accepted by everyone. If Master wasn't accepted by everyone, how then, can I be accepted by all? On the path to eternal damnation shall men find themselves, for forcing their opinions upon others, desiring that their opinions would be accepted by all and claiming to speak for the whole world.

I felt the need to return home to spend time with Mother. I was not sure the loss of her husband was my fault. I sought to compare the pain of losing a husband to the pain of losing a father even though I am not sure how wise that was. Why was I trying to compare one pain in the world with another?

I'm sure Mother will need her only child to be close by, in times like this when she needed comfort from grief. Losing someone or something dear should rank high among the worst types of pain.

Lies upon lies! Pain shouldn't be compared, to check which ranks top or bottom, for menprocess different feelings ofpaininunique ways. The pain one should be entirely concerned about was that of being condemned to eternal damnation. I felt that this was the path for most beings, as it was rare for me to find anyone as perfect as Master among humans.

I arrived home, much to my own displeasure, for I came at a time of mourning. I had left home in search of what I could call mine, in search of better things. I was slowly getting them yet I knew there was no place like home; no matter how big or small one's home is. When I had moved into my house, my corner, I sought to recreate it into a home by inserting features from Father's house.

I failed at that but I wouldn't desire my corner to become like this home I found myself in, at the moment. This home was filled with emotions whichmy mindstruggled to comprehend: pain, wailing, anguish and uncertainty. Whenever a person leaves the earth, people filled the air with crying, anguish and pain rather than rejoicing that one was being born into eternal life.

I found it unpalatable to be in a house of mourning. One must be afraid of the unknown, in this house. Who's next to be taken by the spirit of death? No one knew.

You could also tell that the spirit of fear resides here. One must strive to control his doubts or fears, as to whether he was worthy to live or whether he was next to die. I could tell that many yearned to keep their lives but I must tell you that, 'Whoever desired to save his life will lose it but whoever loses his life for Master's sake will find it.'

Well, who's ready to lose his life while not being sure about what to find next? I must tell you, many were rising who would be willing to lose their lives for Master and for the sake of the world.

This home, once filled with hope, was now something I doubt I could bear for long. I had come to comfort Mother and be by her side. However, she already had so many comforters that I felt I wasn't needed. After all, I was the worst at comforting people; for I believed that everyone has to fight their battles alone.

I am not sure that Mother's comforters did a good job, though. It was not that they were the best, either. They tried, based on their own experiences and in their own ways, to comfort Mother. It surprised me that, despite how evil the world is, people still found a way to show their human side, to care for and support others. We must commend those that tried.

After few hours of arriving home, I was quick to take my leave as the wailing tormented my soul and I couldn't tell the mourners to be quiet. It was a place of mourning and many people could express their emotions in various ways. I concluded within me that I must return to my corner where I could find solace.

How could I tell Mother that I was leaving? I had to summon courage. I wondered how she would feel.

'Mother, I think I have to go,' I said.

'How come? You just arrived,' she replied.

'It's urgent,' I continued.

I didn't expect that she would flare up but she did.

'You little bastard! You killed your father and now you want to kill me?'

I couldn't utter another word. Why would she think that? Onlookers tried to calm her down to avoid further tongue-lashing. It was bad that she thought of me as a killer.

I haven't seen her in such an aggrieved state. It must have been the anguish of losing her husband that was about to make her lose herself. Now, her son, who was expected to be by her side was about to leave.Oh, what pain could do to someone!

I forgave her for what she said. Now, I was becoming like Master who was quick to forgive the sins of the world. As I left our home, what she said dawned on me. I was indeed a killer and I had deceived myself about my ways, so I could forget the truth.

On my way out, I met Miriam and Sophia. Was that a coincidence? Having once been the comforter to Miriam, I was now the afflicted and Miriam would seek to comfort me. It was surprising, for me, to see Sophia with Miriam. It dawned on me at this moment, that the reason Sophia didn't join in the revolt, when I worked at SSC, was because she was friends with Miriam.

It feels like there will be no knowing of me in times to come, for if Mother has lashed out at me in a manner that seemed like she never knew me, then nobody else must know me. How could someone claim to know me if Mother didn't know me? Yes, I did make lots of mistakes when I was younger; who didn't? I wasn't old now but I seemed to have matured.

The fact that I shall fade off the hearts of men, in time to come, made me terrified. Despite my fortune now, my worst insecurity was being myself. I couldn't accept myself because of all I have done on earth. How should I accept my evil ways?

Sophia hugged me tightly, much to Miriam's surprise. Why would she hug me, after I had showed a lack of respect as well as apathy towards her? She sought to comfort me at a time when she felt I was afflicted.

In my mind, I felt perfect but I couldn't put the feeling in words. I always lacked words to express the vast knowledge in my mind. Anyone could sense my hesitation as I struggled to put some compelling words together.

My words didn't feel perfect if the listener was neither replying the way I had envisioned him or her to nor displaying the emotions I desired to evoke. On the path to damnation I shall find myself, for desiring to control people.

My cousin, Miriam, was a little younger than me. I would doubt, if someone said she lacked anything. She had the life of abundance that I had always desired. 'Don't cry,' she said to me even though I no plans to cry. I had forced myself, at this moment, to feel much pain so as to let it out. After all, it was the death of Father that caused it. Miriam went in to stay with Mother and Sophia asked to see me sometime later.

As I drove home, I found myself considering whether to kill myself or not. After all, who in the world hasn't considered killing himself or herself; whether consciously or unconsciously? Humans killed themselves, sometimes not in the present, but in the long run. They did this by: eating the wrong food, drinking

the wrong things, smoking, not exercising, not reading, doing what they shouldn't do and not doing what they should do.

I knew that killing myself would cause sorrow upon sorrow for Mother. Itwasjustthat Motherdespisedmeand Iwantedtopayher back. For striving to pay evil with evil, on the path to damnation shall men find themselves. However, it was better to leave vengeance to Master. His ways would be different from those of men.

I thought about driving my car over the bridge but something was holding me back. I was striving to reclaim my sanity, striving to live some more. I laughed at myself. I was sure I wanted to kill myself but I couldn't bring myself to do it. Why do I want to live more, despite claiming that I had lived in pain for long stretches of time?

It dawned on me that, at the point of hopelessness, there was a fading hope that I kept rekindling. At the point of death, many would still desire to live longer. I was surprised that my mind strove to keep me alive; after all, it was my mind that brought about the thought that I should end my life. I realised that the mind could decide something when the body hasn't fully decided, thus leading to various consequences, as unity was indeed important in all that we do.

If my eyes will lead me to damnation, then I must get rid of them. If it would be my legs, I must do the same to them, for it was better that one enter the heavenly paradise as a blind person or a cripple rather than into damnation with a full body. What if my mind was what was leading me to damnation? How can I get rid of it? 'I think, therefore I am,' just as a wise man said. Getting rid of my mind would mean ridding myself of my sanity. Without my sanity, I must question who I was and whether I have any chance of making it to the heavenly paradise that Master had envisioned for His children.

I knew I existed because I could feel myself. I was insane, to an extent, for I knew that rarely would a sane man seek to drive his car off the bridge. Well, no one can ever rid of himself of his mind, for his mind is himself.

I shall change the pattern of my mind from the path of damnation to the path of heavenly paradise, hopefully. My mind was an accumulation of events, thoughts and knowledge from times past, So, if my mind was striving to lead me to drive my car off the bridge, so as to die and be free of this world, then it means I had filled it in times past with things void of hope, positivity and virtue. This means a series of happenings in the past had led me into desiring to hurt myself now. On the path of damnation I shall find myself, for desiring to hurt myself.

For years, I had walked the earth and filled my mind with things void of virtue; much to my own dissatisfaction. I tried to change my ways, only to find myself dabble more into that which I tried to change. I had fallen back to the old ways of living that I was used to but sought to change.

If I built my mind with things void of virtue as the key components, then it means that things void of virtue kept me

sane. Thus, removing the key components of my mind would surely mean I was bound to break down or lose my sanity, at a point. This was because, the other components I wasn't used to, couldn't keep me sane; regardless of whether they had virtue or not.

Oh, what did I fill my mind with? It must be a culmination of things that I have been through in the past, which made me seek what is without virtue as a priority and to find comfort in it, while giving less or no attention to virtuous things.

I struggled to get a full view of light but my mind would divert my efforts and fill it with darkness. What if I changed the key components of my mind to another thing, to a new thing? It would take a while for my mind to fully come to terms with it, to fully grasp its functions. Whatever I felt I could do with grit and focus without patience, self-control and perseverance, would surely break down. This which I sought to do, would require things of my old mind to hold it together, like they used to.

The human heart tends to conform to that which it already knows. It tends to find sanity in darkness as well as in light. If there was no such thing as good or bad, how could I believe that my virtue would lead me to heavenly paradise? If the good was bound to die early, just as the bad, and those who did good were bound to live longer just as the bad, then I must feel that there's no reward for being good or bad.

Men should always strive for virtue, without desiring something in return. This would ease my doubts concerning the elusive heavenly paradise that my mind has yearned for, for I couldn't tell whether my evil ways would lead me to damnation or heavenly paradise.

Knowledge in the world has presumed that I came from somewhere and I must return somewhere. If, in between all this intertwining of knowledge, I had doubts about the existence of the heavenly paradise that I yearned for, then I am likely to incur Master's wrath which will surely lead me on the path to damnation. This was my opinion, just as many others will have their opinions.

I felt that every opinion that someone has, that is forced on another person, will find its way to the path of damnation. This is because one person was seeking to compel another person to believe his or her own truth. However, I believed that each person should always find his or her own truth.

I had gotten to my cornor safely, after killing the thoughts of suicide. I believed that Master or some higher supernatural being wanted me to live a little longer on earth.

I do not blame those who took their lives because of the misfortune or pain they experienced; misfortune or pain caused by oneself or the world. it was their destiny to take their lives, as Master would always beam from above on those He desired, to save them even at the point of hopelessness. I must, again, say a prayer for the dead, for Father and for us all that shall soon

die. After all, centuries ago, many people had sought to live forever and many had deceived people by dangling an elixir of immortality before those who desired it.

Foolishness and, sometimes, man's lack of knowledge would cause humans to be punished. On the path to damnation shall men who desire immortality and continuity find themselves, for the world was meant to be lived in cycles; as there was a time for everything under the sun.

It wasn't long after I had returned to my corner that someone knocked. I wasn't expecting anyone. Was someone spying on me?

'Who's there?' I asked.

'Why don't you open to see who it is?' the voice replied. It sounded familiar, feminine and lovely. I opened the door and I saw Sophia.

I wasn't expecting her. How did she know where I lived? Who directed her? I stood for a while, contemplating whether or not to let her in, but I couldn't resist her aura.

I had opened up the doors of my soul to a stranger, opened up my corner to one whose intentions I barely knew. She had arrived, meaning that it was destined to arrive and nothing could be done about it. She followed me home because she wanted to, not because Miriam requested it; that was what Sophia said to me.

I offered her a drink which she declined. There were many questions I desired to ask her, some of which I knew the answer to. I went on to ask her the questions, which she answered with endless smiles. These smiles would brighten me up and then infuriate me, thus making me seek to repress my emotions. This was because I was in dire need of female company but lied to myself that I wasn't.

She stared deeply into my eyes, like she was looking for answers from times past, and this made me restless. My restlessness became evident in that I would leave her presence and walk to another part of the house. Believe me, she would swiftly follow me.

Sophia kept on telling me stories which I wasn't sure were to make me either happy or sad. Why would she tell me about her broken family and talk about her life, as if it was what I wanted to hear? Maybe Sophia wanted to be heard by another being; she must have the desire to love or be loved. Maybe she was lonely like me and needed company; after all, my life had many stories I had not told to anyone.

She just couldn't understand what was going through my mind. My mind yearned for peace which Sophia couldn't offer. My mind was neither present with nor absent from her.

She had invaded my corner. How could another being exercise power over me? She bored me with every word that came out of her mouth while at the same time, getting me rooted in her presence without having any desire to leave. Oh, how men will leave you entranced in their presence when you spend time with them! I was going insane; there were no words in my mouth and there were no images in my mind.

I needed to flee her presence but I didn't know how to. I was continually finding new reasons to remain in her presence. My mind was again working outside my will; making me desire to spend more time with Sophia without seeking my opinion. I was fully taking in all her words and actions, something I was angry with myself for doing. After all, nobody knew what's at the bottom of the deep well called the human mind. All that could be seen is what's on the surface or what is shown.

Inmyfinalanalysis, Iwasbeginningtohavealittleunderstanding of her. It was dawning on me that she loved me and I respected her desires to go for what she loved. However, I was angry with myself because I couldn't love her; especially not in the very least, the way she loved me. I must, unfortunately, break her heart.

I hoped my tears would flow if I succeeded in telling her that I couldn't love her. She said she loved me for how I behaved and not for my fortune. However, I had varying personalities and never expected anyone to love me; especially now when I have my fortunes and many will seek to love me.

I had deemed myself unworthy of love in time past. This always found a way into reality. I sought to cut off whomever had come to profess their love to me; I had deemed them unworthy of me.

How could I tell another being that I couldn't love her, despite her love for me? How should I tell the truth, if it was bound to be accompanied by intense pain? I must say, no one is looking for painful truths. Now, I must tell a lie; a beautiful comforting lie, to Sophia that I did love her.

It was getting dark. I wondered if she would decide to spend the night at my place but she didn't ask to sleep over, initially. We never agreed she would.

'Oh, Sophia, I think you have to go now.' I said to her.

Her bright face suddenly switched. It had anger written all over it. Her eyes were red and she started crying as she stood up, seeking to run out of my house. I didn't know what to say to her, any further. I tried to hold her but she pushed me away and I stood in silence. Seeing Sophia angry and crying had destroyed all the sense of peace and happiness, that I had acquired so far, from her.

'I shall not forgive you for this,' she said.

It was my mind, my evil mind, that caused this. It had succeeded again in causing anguish and pain to a beautiful creature like Sophia. Earlier, it succeeded in keeping me alive and helping me lie to Sophia; professing my love to her. She had smiled and kissed me when I said I loved her. I didn't love Sophia, but in an intimate moment with her, I felt so much happiness while forgetting the death of Father and the pains caused by what Mother said to me. I had desired that the moment would not end but my evil mind has come again to ruin any sense of happiness that I felt. In a flash, my evil mind was again scrambling to my brain; seeking to piece together some words that couldn't be spoken and seeking any answers that it could find. Answers to what?

I told Sophia that she had to go and she couldn't hold her anger in. I wondered what would have happened, if I had said to her that I never loved her. Maybe it won't have gotten to that awkward moment when she had cried and fled from my presence. I did the opposite of what someone in love would do to one they loved.

If I had told her earlier that I never loved her, she wouldn't have expected love from me. She would not have been so hurt when asked to leave. Again, I felt the need to kill myself for having caused pain to someone. On the path to damnation shall people find themselves, for lying to another being; to please them with lies.

She took her bag and ran away from my presence. I chased her for a while. I later stopped. The damage had been done. I wanted to give her a ride back home but she wanted nothing from me, I guessed.

I went back to my corner; pondering on the mistakes I had made and the wrath of Master which I shall incur for failing to love another like myself. I couldn't tell whether I loved myself; owing to the fact that I failed to love another.

I would scream out Sophia's name at different times in the night. Probably, another man in the same situation would have found a way to steer clear without causing pain to another being. Why couldn't I love a beautiful creature like Sophia, despite the fact she was willing to go to great lengths to make me love her? Maybe I did love Sophia; owing to the fact that I felt happiness and peace in her presence, coupled with pain for hurting her.

Why couldn't I bring myself to love or to show love? Perhaps, I couldn't love due to my past mistakes, experiences and trauma which made me believe I would always cause pain to people. On the path to damnation I shall find myself, for not fully loving the heart of men.

I slept off, thinking about Sophia, and dreamt of her. Sometimes, our desires, events or experiences would find ways to get into our dream state. I experienced perfect love with her in my dream. Unconsciously, I found refuge in my dreams. For how long would it be, before the unconscious state of my dream or the conscious state of my corner (in both I found solace) would become a nightmare? It would torment me, as it would become impossible for me to understand how a being like me could change the state of things in which another being found themselves.

What hope is there for the future if one dares not dive into the past, to fully grasp one's mistake, learn from it, let go and make plans not to repeat it? After all, without my past, I wouldn't have arrived at the present I found myself. Remember, I was an accumulation of my past experiences, thoughts, events and knowledge. My future self played little or no role in what I had turned out to be, at this moment.

I would seek to find myself, because only then can I help to find others. Many kept searching in the world to find themselves, seeking different things, seeking to know who they are. If men couldn't find who they are after endless trials, they would be tormented by their failures.

I desired to numb the pain I felt. It was the same pain I had caused to Mother, Sophia and all who had loved me. I wished I had not met them at all so I wouldn't cause any of them pain. It wasn't so, in reality. It was paramount that I met them; it was destined that this moment would happen and that I caused pain to them all. Without my parents, I would not be born. Without Mother, there will be no knowing of me and perhaps, if Josephine had accepted and loved me perfectly, then I would be loving to Sophia.

It would dawn on me that, in all these moments, my mind was fixed on the wrong things. This made me feel that, sometimes, humans remember the wrongs more than the right.

Do you remember when I stated earlier, that humans are connected and that they improve one another? Sometimes, we desire to improve ourselves for the sake of another being. I fantasised, sometimes, about the beings of the world. I did this, to the extent that they became the object of my pain and happiness.

I was obsessed with some people, for various reasons. There were some who inspired me to come up higher, as well as higher-ups who did not want to have anything to do with me; for they felt I had not acquired the knowledge they had. They cast me away, as they would do to one of the worst or lowly.

It was a selfish world we found ourselves in. In times past, I sought to acquire knowledge so as to endear myself to those whose acceptance I craved. I also sought knowledge from my peers and those below me, as anyone and anything could be a source of learning; if you look deeply.

There is a path for everyone, as each person has a role to play by being in the world.

I was obsessed with Josephine in times past, due to the human desire to love and be loved. Sometimes, we would have to conform to the desires of the world rather than those of ourselves. To me, it felt right for each human to find love in himself or herself; and not in another being.

In times past, I lived just to please people, so as to be free of the pain that they caused me because I was among the lowly in the world. I endlessly desired to fit into their world.

Maybe I should appreciate people for helping me grow, for developing me into a better or worse person. However, I couldn't tell whether it was so; for all the knowledge I had acquired, while desiring to please men, has gone a long way in bringing me to my present state.

Sometimes, our knowledge will not save us as I yearned for someone to stir me up. I yearned for Sophia's love, for I was in the worst state that I could find myself, and desired the bliss that previously came from her presence. On the path to damnation I shall find myself, for failing to take the opportunity given to me by Master, or by the world, to find love in a human; as I doubted if I could truly live in the world without love.

Is everyone assigned to a particular field of life? If anyone labours the most in a field that isn't his or her ordained one, he or she may find it hard to get to the top. This was even though there was nothing easy in the world of men; neither in living nor in dying.

People found the same things either easy or hard. I must now doubt myself, when I said there is nothing one can't achieve without a certain grit and focus. One must have conceived the expected achievement mentally, before seeing it come to reality.

If the mind is willing, is the body willing to work with it, also? Will both be ready to cooperate, to walk a certain path of hardship for a time, so as to learn and hopefully achieve something one is not sure will become a reality? Patience and perseverance were advisable requirements but, sometimes, they would lead a person -who was waiting for a reality that may never come - to damnation. These qualities made such people to ignore and fail to explore other things that could go right for them, because they were waiting on something that seemed guaranteed.

Another person will seek to have faith and hope in what they desired to achieve; despite not knowing where it shall lead. That shall be for another person to answer, as I shall try to rid myself of the present situation and thinking that I found myself.

I had come to believe that, once I had grown and become free, I would quickly comprehend the human heart. This would never be so. I must ask why it is that, two people who worked the same way and followed the same routine did not get the same results, at the end. Shall we find something to blame or shall we say that Master`s will was being done in their lives? I must tell you, I felt it was Master's will that I get to this level and have this fortune as well as all that I had at this point.

On the other hand, another set of two men who worked in different ways can achieve the same desired result. There could be a variety of reasons for one failing where one was expected to succeed. Well, every disappointment and failure would create another path. Here I was, seeking to advise men to accept whatever came their way fully; regardless of merit (whether they deserved it or not). On the path to damnation I shall find myself, for seeking to help and advise others while I couldn't help and advise myself to pull me out of the situation I found myself.

If everything the world has to offer was placed before someone and he or she couldn't tell what he or she wanted, it could be that such a person either sought nothing or desired so many things that he or she couldn't be sure of what he or she truly wanted. All in all, things would constantly elude man. This applies to me, as well, Peace will elude me, for all the evil I have done, even if I have temporarily found it in times past from Sophia.

My corner had been a safe haven, for a while. It was a place where I always found peace and serenity, in a world filled with evil and much uncertainty. It was my defence mechanism; an

escape route from the turmoil and busyness in the world. After all, everyone sought to escape various things that tormented and haunted them. However, there are some things one can't escape.

How long would it be, before my soul and mind got so familiar with my corner, that it found a way to make it torment and haunt me? How long, before the escape route of my corner closes and I start to yearn endlessly for another to open and be a safe haven to me?

Can people be truly satisfied with one particular thing? It was like a businessman who has made quite a fortune from crude oil, who realised that something new was coming and his oil won't always be appreciated. In another instance, it was also like a lover who has become so familiar with one that he feels that the love can no longer evolve. In both cases, wouldn't the people want something new? Everyone wanted something more than or different from what they had. Men always loved variety. At some point, things that held a person together will no longer do so. An example was my safe haven.

People did what they deemed fit, under the watchful eyes of Master. Master also did whatever He deemed fit, with the world. For instance, how was it that Master would love one and hate the other, in the case of a set of twins in the womb of a woman? An insane man would seek to question Master on His very decision to love one and hate another. I would seek to be on the side of the insane man, to question Master, for I had endless questions to ask Master. However, I would be terrified to do that; for I could incur Master's wrath in time to come. How could the created question the creator?

I believed that Master loved me, despite my sufferings and failure. However, how could Master love a doubtful being like me? I had yearned for the cup of life to pass over me but it wasn't my choice that would prevail; as I still lived in the world. It was the will of Master that would prevail, as I shall seek to clear my doubt by increasing my faith.

On the path to damnation I shall findmyself, for thinking Master's love is only for a season, for a selected group of people and for those with faith. Nothing can separate us from the love of Master. However, if Master loved one and hated another, then I must do the same. On the path to damnation shall one find himself, for seeking not to love all as he did himself. If one didn't love himself, how can he love another? We can't give what we don't have, so one must learn to love oneself before one could love another.

Ever since Sophia ran from my corner, I began to grow increasingly depressed and full of despair whenever I was in it. I could feel her presence all over, like Master who is always with me but whom I couldn't see. I could feel her tears and the pain that I caused her. Feeling Sophia's presence in my corner made me restless. It was like someone was after me. I wondered how Sophia could have much power over my mind, as it played endless tricks on me. It was beginning to dawn on me that Sophia was the source of the restlessness and unease I felt in my corner.

I had the feeling of loneliness whenever I arrived in my corner, from any outing, because Sophia won't be mine. This was even though I never wanted her. How could my mind make me feel that I wanted her? I could be out in the world and buy love for myself, but what's the need of buying love in the world if I don't feel a thing? My failure at accepting Sophia's love tormented me, such that I found no peace in my corner where peace and serenity once reigned.

I stayed out late, just to make sure I found something that kept me from retuning to my corner where I received endless torments because of Sophia. I desired to summon courage to fight that which tormented me but I couldn't. The truth was that, I was a weakling like most people who found means to appear strong.

People found ways to escape the battles in their lives. I spent more time at the bar to escape my corner that now tormented me. I desired to be with a company that was not meant for me. I was surprised at how I seemed to find a certain kind of peace by being with this company of men. Sometimes, your mind would seek to make you feel better in situations that should have made you worse, so it will find rest from something else that troubled it.

I was in a company of men who knew only how to drink and, in between, get to smoke. However, I could only drink; though that was against my will. This was because I felt that smoking would cut my life short. It seemed too risky and I felt better being called a drunkard rather than a smoker. A fool I was, for thinking I would live long by indulging in one shameless act rather than indulging in another.

Despite all this, there was a certain feeling that I knew what I had to do but I failed to do it. The fact that I failed to smoke, but drank at will, brought the thought to my mind quickly that man will surely die of something. I could die of my drinking, another will die of his smoking; and another who smokes and drinks won't die of smoking or drinking but of something else entirely.

Was it a bad idea that I found myself at the bar, seeking to dull my senses, despite knowing what to do to free myself of the torments of my corner? I could see vivid pictures of Sophia in my mind. I must be a fool for calling the acts of drinking and smoking, which were escape routes for some people, a shameless act.

It was strange to be with these people at the bar. I did not think I ever dreamt of a day like that, but now I had become part of them for the time being; after all, there was a time for everything.

'There would always be a bright idea,' said one of them. I knew that it will be wasted, for they wouldn't act on it. This was perhaps due to lack of resources or their ignorance. However, my being here means I soaked up all the knowledge and ideas of these bright wasted minds who found a certain kind of joy from living a low life, unlike me who desired the high life in the world. Didn't they desire to change and go higher? With these ideas, these men should have their place at the top in the world; but they can't and they won't, for they shall not act on them.

I had come to the bar, not to be like them, but to escape from myself and my corner. I found some bright ideas that were being thrown away and wasted by men. With the fortune I had, I knew I could buy their souls and their minds. Here, I was willing to buy men's souls and mind for myself; yet I have not bought mine because I believed it belonged to another. After all, I had become of the world; which means my soul and mind should belong to the world as well.

Sometimes, in the world, something you expect will be given to someone else, what you own will be taken from you while something you think you don't deserve will be given to you. This was the world where something I hated might become my greatest joy, something that tormented me would trigger me to take a corresponding decision. If not for Sophia, I wouldn't have found myself at this bar where I was seeking to acquire the knowledge and ideas that this company of low-life men had in them. On the path of damnation I shall find myself, for calling beautifully and wonderfully creatures created by Master lowlifes. They only needed to be intoxicated, to claim that they felt intense focus.

Knowledge and ideas came from Master or the devil. Perhaps, they were nurtured. However, I would feel that Master or the devil must have directed one to find the knowledge in something or somewhere. How could Master give such knowledge and ideas to one of these men who would never act on them? Welcome to the world where knowledge as well as ideas were wasted and purpose was not actualised. On the path of damnation shall men find themselves, for not using the knowledge, ideas and talents given to them by Master or the devil.

I must tell you, it was never going to be easy to soak up knowledge of low-lifers as it felt intertwined with the knowledge I had accrued over time. I must beware so that, in the desire to soak up knowledge from the low-lifers, I did not finally become like them. I wanted to avoid being influenced by and becoming like some beings that I was better than.

I couldn't bring myself to become one with something I haven't fully processed and understood. If I soaked up their ideas without acting on them, then, in time to come, I was bound to become like them - having wasted talents and ideas. On the path to damnation I shall find myself, if it were to be so.

Maybe, in my foolishness, I thought I belonged with this group of low-lifers. That was what a voice began to say to me. Was it not the same voice that was to help me put this knowledge into actions that was telling me I belonged to a group of wasted talents and low-lifers? I should have known that, once I found pleasure in something and a means to escape the reality that I found myself in, my mind would find it hard to let go.

After all, why would I want to sacrifice a place of pleasure in which I found myself (which was the bar) for the torment I shall find in my corner? However, the life of endless pleasure in which I find myself now might lead me to damnation. I was becoming so obsessed with having this pleasure that, when I woke up sober the next morning, my senses would fully return

and seek to show me that I was still stuck in the reality I wanted to escape from. I would become fully aware and seek to discern the knowledge as well as ideas accrued from the previous night.

Once the sun rose, I would find myself becoming restless until I visited the bar. The desire to visit the bar never came directly but I could tell the desires my mind planned not to show. I could already decipher what it wanted. I had been betrayed by my mind, as it tempted and tricked me into doing something without actually telling me to do so.

I knew that being away from my corner and out in the world was going to lead me to stray. However, with an underlying desire, I wanted that; as I wanted to feel something different. I didn't mean to fail whenever I was out in the world, but tell me, did anyone mean to fail? I always wanted to survive, to succeed; but the fear of failing would surely find its way to my mind, whether I was winning or not.

I must ponder the meaning of the words, `Enjoy your youthful days` without driving myself to insanity. I can't call myself sane, as my mind always drove me to do what it wanted. I felt I was no longer in control of myself, as it took me to the bar against my will and afterwards left me in despair. It left me to, again, separate what's right from wrong and to sort out the knowledge I had accrued from the men I met at the bar.

Should I blame myself for the endless stops in this journey, that life has forced on a fragile being like me? These stops forced me to feel many things and to make mistakes, without seeking to correct me. I had become terrified to make another mistake, yet I found myself living as if I felt no longer in control of myself and my mind. I remembered vividly that I gave advice to others; the same advice that I was incapable of following. I must forgive myself if, in the heat of the moment, I forgot which side I'm on; as I had waged another war within me.

Tell me, how can the created suddenly wage war with its creator? On the path to damnation shall my mind find itself, for causing troubles within me. I aspired to be free of this mess that I found myself in. How can I find myself fighting against powers of my mind which I should have dominion over? What's the need of fighting against something if you were bound not to win? I can't have the thought of being weak or of losing battles, on my mind. On the path to damnation I shall find myself, for being weak.

I must cry to myself, if these torments of the mind continued, that I endlessly yearned for peace. What if I could never find peace, either within me or in my fellow humans? What if peace was imaginary and only existed in a fantasy world created inside my head, such that I could no longer find solace in it; as it waged war on its creator? What if peace was never permanent but only a temporary achievement that men got for themselves or for others? Time and again, a cycle will occur that will spring up a revolt and make peace vanish,

In the world in my head, my very own creations would war against their creator. I was deeply surprised at how they came to know about warring when I had created them to only know and bring peace to me. If I rid them of freewill, will they get it again somehow, so as to go against my wishes? They fought for their freedom even though they never lived in bondage.

When the created seeks to wage war against its creator, then something was wrong. It was just like one seeing right in a placed filled with wrong, one seeking to give voice to a voiceless being and man waging war against their creator; against Master, by seeking to do opposite of what He expected of us. Then, I must demand that Master rids us of freewill. Maybe somehow, we can get it against Master's wishes.

If Master knows it all, then everything that happened was bound to happen. If that was the case, how could one dangle the idea of freewill before a being that did not have it? If I was here; then I was meant to be here. On the path to damnation I shall find myself, for questioning Master's authority and claiming the world was void of freewill.

I don't think people consciously seek to incur the wrath of Master. I don't think man will ever want to experience the sight of war. I don't think anyone who ever experienced war or lived in times of war will want to experience it again.

Father told me the stories of wartime. He was a soldier who had grown up, with fear becoming a part of him. I think Father suffered Post- Traumatic Stress Disorder. However, he found a way to keep himself together, as well as to show love and care for his family. No one would want to experience a particular traumatic experience or pain the second time. However, it would not always be so; as many would re-experience the same trauma or pain that they sought never to re-experience, whether by conscious or unconscious means.

If people do not want war, how come peace eludes us? As I have always said, some people fed on chaos to achieve their desires. If the kingdom of heaven suffered violence and the violence takes it by force, then I believe that some things are meant to end in violence so as to achieve what is desired.

Sometimes, in an unexplained moment of fear or pain, I would be quick to scream the name of Master or various other spiritual beings that men believe in. I shall then began to pray for myself, despite my lack of strong belief in Master. I also desired to pray for those like me, who were fighting a battle of the mind, as well as those in a real war zone.

I must question this. When one calls unto Master for mercy and help, in a troubled time, if Master does not come to their aid, should one say Master is unjust or that He does not relate to our pain?

Were the occurrences at His crucifixion not a show of the pain He felt? Would one say that Master doesn't feel any pain, so it made it impossible for Him to come to our aid when we are in pain and needed Him the most? How could one explain the full workings of Master? I couldn't tell, as I only spoke for myself. I could not understand the full workings of Master.

Ifwe are His sons andnotsubjects or slaves, thentell me if it is right that a son requests bread and the father gives him a stone. Is it right that a needy child shall call upon Master and He shall ignore him? If men, despite being evil, know how to give good gifts to their children, why then shall Master who is in heaven not give good gifts to His children? Many desired good gifts from Master and it seemed that He did not hearken unto them, but was silent in their time of need. I watched parents do evil to their children; abusing them, killing them, leaving them with trauma and no proper training on how to to cope in the world of men.

If I was made in the image of Master, then He must feel pain; and especially the pain I felt. I begin to question our need for Master, if He would not hear us or come to our aid when we needed Him. Would it be better if we sought no help from Master? I must tell you, those who sought no help from Master are closer to damnation; for how can one live in the world without Master? How could someone get far in life with absolutely no knowledge on how to request help from Master or fellow humans?

Master would feel so close some times and yet very far in times of need. Come to think of it, who am I? Who am I to question the ways of Master, as He will have compassion and mercy on whomever He deems fit? If, in times of war and need, Master was silent, then some will be sacrificed for others to live. In a moment of desperation, I had prayed to be among those not sacrificed;

despite having sacrificed someone to get to this level I found myself.

The events in the world of men were all connected. My entire life's journey was connected; from the past to the present to the future. I couldn't tell where it led me. I put everything into my search; the search to make the pain go away. What pain? I couldn't even explain the pain I felt. I desired peace, as it could give me control over myself. I must find control, even if it keeps eluding me. If everything was meant to elude me, then I must be sure that I wasn't of this world. How could I be in a world where everything eludes me? I had my fortune but it couldn't save me from everything.

I should desire to be of another world, perhaps of the heavenly paradise in which everything that eludes me on earth shall be given unto me. Only in dying shall one see the world of heavenly paradise; a world I wasn't sure of getting to because of my iniquities on the earth. It was a world that I felt no man on earth was sure to be part of.

Suddenly, I would think of Mother and all the sweet souls in the world; many whom are still hidden, that would be on the path of heavenly paradise. They wouldn't find themselves on the path of damnation that I found myself. The thought of Mother brought an added motivation to me, to be better, so as to force myself on the path to heavenly paradise. Thus, it suddenly dawned on me that men truly improve each other.

Chapter Fourteen

What would men do, to be free? People would sacrifice anything for their own satisfaction and, sometimes, for the satisfaction of others. Some days in the world evoke different feelings, when compared to others.

On a chilly morning when the sunlight was not fully visible, a dim light found a way into my corner to dry up my skin. The sun will seek to wax stronger, to radiate its powers so as to give full light to the world. The sun will make sure it doesn't forget its duty to the world. On some days, I don't even know my duty to the world. On other days, it would feel like I'm filled with a sense of purpose.

On this particular day, it seemed that the weather triggered me to see a glimpse of my duty to the world. This duty was to serve, to be the best version of myself, to make peace and to have a sense of courage to call Sophia! Oh, how random things in the world could be the inspiration needed to do something!

I had thought, for long, about the perfect words to say to her. My mind has been so filled with the disorders of my daily life that I found it hard to piece together a few good words to say to Sophia. I was angry with myself and filled with anguish, as I failed to find the right words.

I would desire to find ways to stop thinking about Sophia, for if the hearts of men can not be fully pleased, how could I expect to please Sophia? On the path to damnation I shall find myself, for failing to make peace and reconcile my differences with beings of the world.

At past seven in the night, a certain desire to see Mother arose in me. it had been a few weeks since I last saw her. The thoughts of staying in my corner troubled me and the once irresistible desire to visit the bar vanished. Of course, I knew there's an end to everything in the world. I felt that I could no longer imbibe any knowledge from the men at the bar and if I went on visiting the bar, it may spell the end of me.

Also, I thought about Mother and the fact that our last meeting did not end well. Driving to her house brought about the same odd feelings of time past, when I felt that everything that happened was my fault. I presumed that, if I had done things a little better, Father might still be alive and Mother will be happy with me.

I always desired peace, and sought to make peace with those I have hurt as well as those that hurt me. I sometimes took the blame, whether it was mine or not. Death was inevitable, so it was destined that Father will die. Maybe I desired to evade death just so I could disappear from this world, just like few who didn't experience death in this world but were taken to heavenly paradise.

I caused pain to Mother, which was not the beautiful pain she must have felt from giving birth to me. I knew I was bringing myself to damnation rather than to heavenly paradise but I was still in the world because Master has deemed me fit to live. He was giving me another chance to right my wrongs and make the most of my stay in the world. This was another chance I felt I would end up wasting.

Why would Master give me a chance to live on, in my sinful ways? It was probably in the hope that I will change. This was something I was beginning to doubt. I must again question Master's intention, in the long run, to let me live in the world. This was because I accumulated more questions without answers to come.

Despite my desire to ascend to heavenly paradise, I was scared of dying; which showed that I wasn't ready to leave the world despite my clamour not to live in it. If I lived for Master in the world, dying was even better, for I shall gain more.

How can I live fully in the present, while endlessly thinking of the future or the end of myself? What's the essence of thinking about the future of myself, if I had no say on whether I would wake up tomorrow or not? Despite my doubts, I hoped that everything will work out for my good so I can finally find some answers in the world.

I arrived at Mother's house and a lot of people were there, even though it was night. They were there to pay their condolences, even though it had been weeks since Father died. It was presumed that a place of mourning was better than a place of partying, for death is the destiny of everyone, so the living should take this to heart.

If the afflicted was meant to be comforted, why wasn't Mother getting any comfort or feeling better? She lay down and her voice sounded cranky. This was not typical of her. One could tell that she was worn out and I could sense that she was on a tight rope. The death of Father surely hurt her, unlike me who showed little emotions. The mental toil of losing Father began to show physically, on Mother.

Indeed, everything was connected. Mother seemed to have it together at one moment and, in another moment, she had an outburst. She would roll on the ground, crying, while people held her. She would say she needed to die, complaining of a headache and fever. She complained of everything.

Why would anyone seek to incur the wrath of Master? Did she even care about the consequences of her words? If Mother

should die, I would be severely lonely. Even though I was lonely at the moment, I had people who could go out of their ways for my sake. However, pushing away so many people meant that the number of these people was dropping. I even had fears concerning Mother`s intention towards me, for she believed I hurt her.

Mother lay on the bed, later that night. Her complaints of pain as well as tiredness, propelled me to take her to the hospital after several relatives insisted I did. On arriving at the hospital, I tried to escape bureaucracy that came with a place like that. The fact that Mother's case wasn't an emergency meant that the hospital staff would likely delay before attending to her, for the country I found myself in did not entirely care about its citizens.

Should I bypass the orderly cultured manner in which things were meant to be done? Should I jump the queue? I have the fortune now, which signified it was easier and faster for Mother to see the doctors, compared to those who had arrived much earlier than me. I could easily buy into the demands that men desired. I must hate myself, though I should pity the poor. This was because their lack of fortune would mean that men of the world would despise them for their wretchedness and seek to overrun them for their own desires as well as reasons.

How would I make the poor, that had come before me to the hospital, understand that Mother was precious to me? The factthat they had come to the hospital meant they weren't ready to die, as they were precious and whoever they brought to see the doctor would be precious to them.

I should get rid of the thought of intimidating the poor with my fortune or whatever means necessary, for this would bring me closer to damnation.

All of a sudden, in a distance, I saw someone in white scrubs. She was a beautiful tall creature; one I believed was sent from Master, one that immediately stirred something inside of my soul. I couldn't get my eyes away from her and my mind to stop imagining things about her. I knew I must speak with her, with a boldness that was not typical of me.

The biggest obstacle I had tried to overcome, so far in my life, has been my mind. In this situation, it was acting like it had in times past; seeking to help me. It was a hospital and one could come up with something to say to someone. Comforting words, I believed, were the best words to say to one in an hospital.

I walked up to the lady in white. I told her about Mother as well as the fact that Father was no more. I needed to trigger her emotions. After all, no matter how evil one is, one would always have a soft spot. I was willing to give her a tip, to increase my chances and aid my desire for her to do my bidding, but I hesitated. To my surprise, she volunteered to book an appointment with the doctor immediately. As she left my presence, I stood fixated in the moment and looked at her until she entered a room nearby.

I sat down with Mother, still wondering what a beautiful heart the lady in white had. My fortune couldn't save me in this instance, for if I had offered it to this beautiful lady, she may not

have accepted it. If she did accept, I would be setting her on the path to damnation and pulling her away from Master whom I believed she was sent from.

Shouldn't we all believe that we all are sent from Master? A fool I was, for I was already drawing her away from Master by convincing her to book an appointment with the doctor for Mother; so we could see the doctor earlier than those who had arrived before us.

The circumstances I found myself in propelled my boldness to heights I thought unimaginable, in times past. I felt in perfect unity with myself, because of this beautiful lady. My fortune and the boldness I seemed to have found spurred me to do things that used to frighten me, like making peace with others. However, I could not leave Mother just yet; in the bid to recover lost things or times. with my fortune and new found boldness.

The beautiful lady came back. She requested that I and Mother follow her. I would finally take a look at the badge she wore. It read, 'Nurse Gabriela.' I must control the way I looked at her now, for I couldn't look at her confidently before now when I felt in perfect unity within myself.

I sought to prevent my thoughts from taking me far into the recesses of her soul and body. I tried to remain in the present, even though hospitals did give me the creeps. However, meeting a beautiful lady like Gabriela meant that I hoped to see more of her; which was, of course, by staying In the hospital. On the path to damnation I shall find myself, for desiring to stay in hell while having the hope to see heaven later on.

We saw the doctor, who instructed that Mother be admitted so that tests could be run on her. I was fine with this, even though she was not. She preferred to be taken home, to recuperate. Mother was given a bed between 2 patients. The bed to the right was occupied by a little boy who, I found out, suffered from appendicitis. He went through excruciating pain which was shown in the way he turned and groaned on the bed. He was waiting to be operated upon.

The bed to the left was occupied by a woman who had suffered a stillbirth.

The doctors performed dilation and evacuation to remove parts of the dead child that were still in her body. I could tell that she was in pain as well, owing to the screaming and gnashing I saw. I began to wonder about the reason for her pain; was this the pain of losing a child or the pain of surgery?

I desired to empathise with both her and the little boy; to find a common ground for their pains. There were endless visitors and sympathisers trooping in, despite it being night time, to see them. One could sense the pain of the parents of the little boy and hope that it would reduce. It was hoped that the boy's pain will be over soon, once he starts to recover.

This was different from the pain of the woman who had lost her child. Some people had children and she couldn't even have one. Mother had one, which was me. I thought about the

stories she told me of the two children she lost, before she had me. I wondered how it happened that they died. I would think about my two siblings who had died and I would again join forces with the woman, who I believe would question Master's intention in the world. Why let her become pregnant in the first place if she was bound to lose the baby? Again, who are we to question the creator who did whatever He desired to the created?

I tried to keep their pain from getting to me, as the thought of losing Mother continued to force its way into my mind. I felt that the pain of losing Mother would be a grievous one for me to feel, as compared to the woman who lost her child. I hoped and prayed that the woman would have another child but no one would replace Mother if she died.

I wish I had the power to get rid of the pain of the patients beside Mother. I felt that they deserved the peace that Master offered. I thought about many in the hospital and in the world, who suffered pain and looked up to Master for various things. Would Master again look down on them from His heavenly throne and be blind to their pains? Would Master leave them in their pain? Would their desires elude them as Master will shut His ears from hearing them?

Doubt will begin to fill up my mind, as I confirmed that this is not a place for me. With Gabriela having left my presence to attend to other patients, this place has turned into a hell-hole and I began to question whether I was truly worthy of being alive. I must seek to escape from this thought, for if I was still alive, then it was destined that I live at this time.

I must find Gabriela; I must seek to see her beautiful face which brought me instant peace and rest. I searched and searched but I couldn'tfindher. Iaskedaboutherand Iwastoldthatshehadgone home because her shift was over. I waited anxiously for another encounter with Gabriela while replaying the short encounters I had with her. The thought of seeing her again made me happy.

I desired to thank Gabriela endlessly, as if she was the saviour of my soul. I forced myself to think only about her, as the midnight drew near. I would desire to see a perfect creature like Gabriela in my dreams. I must seek to kiss her and have her all to myself; never to let her go.

Iwasinthemidstofmyimaginationwhen, allofasudden, screams filled the air. Why would the hearts of men seek to ruin a perfect moment for a creature like me? I rushed to the scene to find that a creature like me had been pronounced dead. Friends and family were crying, seeking to pour out their soul to the air, without getting a reply from Master. Master seemed so far away, despite the fact that He is always with us. The spirit of death had done Master's bidding by taking a creature back to Master for judgement.

I would love to shut them down because they ruined a perfect moment. I would love to cast them out for crying their souls out at such a late hour. However, I couldn't do all of these, as I found a way to calm my anger towards them for ruining the perfect moment I was having.

I must find ways to quiet them down, especially since they had put fear and doubt into other patients. These patients would begin to brace themselves, as they could be the next to die. This is because, sometimes, your faith can't save you and no one could tell what would come next in this world. On the path to damnation I shall find myself for thinking less about the death of a creature like me, just because he or she was not related to me. It was a woman of my age who had died, with so many people surrounding her.

I must allow people to feel the pain of losing their loved ones and let them cry their souls out for another who was no longer on earth. I must say a prayer for her, for her poor soul, in the hope that she will be in heavenly paradise rather than damnation; where many in the world shall find themselves.

I went to Mother, out of a sudden desire to stay close to her. The way our relatives sympathised with her reminded me of Aunt Suzzy and Father's death. I kept blocking thoughts of Mother's imminent death. My irrational beliefs had brought me to the moment in which I filled myself with negativity.

Mother was awake now; she couldn't sleep. She spoke in a slower tone, to which I would always smile and nod, even if I did not hear what she said clearly sometimes. She kept complaining about the hospital and stated that she will like to go back home in the morning. She talked a lot, even on the sickbed. This irked me out but I concealed my annoyance.

She talked about Father as if he was here and I cried at will. I sought to make her feel at ease in anyway I can. She made abrupt demands for food, at a late hour of the night, which she had no appetite for when it came. She complained that she was hot and asked for the air conditioner to be turned up. In a swift moment, she would complain of cold and ask that we turn it down.

In the past few hours, Mother had complained about everything around her. She had become fragile. I and everybody who was with her could sense it. The once strong woman was reduced to a weakling. She was on the verge of breaking apart, never to be fixed; on the verge of dying and never to be saved.

My mind got filled with a pessimistic feeling which I sought to rid myself of. This weird feeling was darkness and there was pain afterwards. I believed that darkness would surely lead one to insanity or damnation, if one dwelt on it for long.

My desire to have Mother recover quickly overcame the torment of thoughts of Sophia.

How come I did not show perfect love and care to Mother, in times past? Did this contribute to her illness? I questioned Master's decision to take Father out of the world, despite knowing that it would have a domino effect on my sweet mother. I questioned myself for seeking to be much closer to Mother at the point of her death that many believed was forthcoming.

No one is truly free, in the human race, for we begin to die immediately we are born. How could we truly live if we are bound to die?

If only Master would again shine His light on Mother, to save and heal her! Maybe my mind would be free of this darkness, which I believed was the imminent death of Mother. And, if it were to happen, I would question why Master knows all things and still lets some things happen in the world. However, sacrifices have to be made as men will never be truly free in the world.

Chapter Fifteen

Only the dead have seen the end of life. I believed that one who has had a near-death experience is likely to avoid questions about the dead. Although not utterly visible, there will be always be a connection between the living and the dead.

Morning will come and, as Mother slept, I sought to escape to my corner because I felt so much unease, being at the hospital. There was no Gabriela at the moment to bring me peace and, surprisingly, I had made Gabriela an object of my peace. I left Mother with our relatives.

I got to my corner where I found a terrifying amount of peace and freedom, which was typical of times past before Sophia had invaded my corner. Even now, thoughts of Sophia still popped up in my head at random times but I blocked them off. The thoughts of Mother and of seeing Gabriela again filled my mind, so I could not dwell on the thoughts of Sophia.

When afternoon came, I went to the hospital to see how Mother was faring, I marvelled at the fact that thoughts of Gabriela still filled my mind. Much to my surprise, Gabriela was the nurse attending to Mother. I just couldn't stop staring at her. What a beautiful creature she was! 'Why must I gush at her beauty?' I wondered to myself, for she wasn't beautiful as compared to Sophia. However, I found instant peace just looking at her. I felt so drawn to her and it was quite obvious, by the way I stared at her. Perhaps, I did love Gabriela.

Her irritation was shown in her bodily reactions. She sought to flee my presence after attending to Mother and I asked to follow her. I thought to assist, maybe by carrying the trays, or to keep her company. On the path to damnation I shall find myself, for trying to derail one off the path meant for her, by seeking to keep her company or to follow her. Due to my actions, one could tell that Gabriela wasn't focused on her job. This resulted in her telling me to take a seat or to go stay with Mother, as she had other patients to attend to and it wasn't right that I follow her around.

I marvelled at how bold I had become. It dawned on me that, when you found something you felt was meant for you, the experience would make you whole and better. Sometimes, I would insist on accompanying Gabriela to see other patients, seek to comfort

other patients, offer some pieces of advice and sometimes even request to pay the bills of some. Oh, how one could make another better without knowing it! My desire to be in Gabriela's presence has resulted in me being bold among humans. I was indeed finding heaven in hell.

One could tell that Gabriela wasn't trying to be rude to me. The rate at which I bothered her would make me scream, if I was in her shoes. However, she was being professional and human After all, her job was to help with healing. A number of patients would seek to believe in the tiniest hope, to back up the desire that healing would come to them soonest. I conjured some hope for myself, believing that this would become a saviour to Mother; healing her in the process.

No one would like to lose a loved one. However, a loved one was lost every minute. Either one better than me or one worse than me will die soon and yet, I lived on. I must come to conclude that, if the thought of losing another loved one was consistent, if my thought of losing Mother became a reality, then I must desire to die as well so as to find and be with that which have been taken from me. I must desire to become one of the dead. I was a fool, for desiring that which I don't fully understand. On the path to damnation I shall find myself, for I shall perish; owing to my lack of knowledge in the world.

Gabriela found a way to give peace to my troubled self. I called her Ella. I wanted to speak with her consistently. Now, I was the one doing the talking; unlike the times I spoke with Sophia and she was always the one doing the talking.

I struggled to find perfect words to say to Ella. I told her stories about myself and few things I have repressed, in times past. I yearned for her presence because I desired the peace I always found from it. There were times where we spoke, in which I believed that Ella repressed her desires towards me. I still felt like a stranger to her because, despite endless plans to work my way to her mind, I couldn't. This was because she was smarter and acted perfectly.

Finally I believed that I had met one without flaws, one whom was perfect. She spoke in a slow bold tone. Her best words were, 'Oh dear,, take a seat and I will get back to you.' This always made me smile rather than get angry.

The doctors diagnosed Mother with coronary artery disease. Perhaps, this was caused by the age factor coupled with the emotional and mental stress she was going through. We had to stay longer in the hospital as Mother wasn't making any progress. She complained endlessly of pain all over her body and that she couldn't sleep properly.

I had not slept at the hospital since the first night because I had come to realise that Ella only worked morning shifts. She worked late the first night because she was covering for someone else. I had to change my visitation times to morning and afternoon so they would correspond with Ella's shifts. I came to the hospital every morning to stay beside Mother who would begin to tell me stories of times past, some that I was shocked to hear.

She told me that Father had hit her. It happened only once and she believed she was the cause; she felt she deserved it. How could she hide such a thing from me? I doubt anyone else knew it; it was her secret. Would this make me hate Father, who was already dead, the more? I pondered why someone could hit the one they claimed to love. Also, how come Mother loved Father so much that she couldn't cope with the grief of losing him? Love, I believed, will be the end of us all.

I might believe that, at one's point of death, one might be enlightened the more. He or she would see the world from a whole new perspective while seeking to make more impact in the world. After all, no one leaves the earth with any belonging. The only thing that's important is what one has left behind.

I found that, being with Mother in this period brought me closer to her; with our bonds deepening. There were times I was at the hospital when Mother was asleep and Ella would be busy that I wouldn't want to discomfort or distract her. I would either walk to the rooftop of the hospital, from which I will gaze out into the world, or sometimes wander into the streets to savour the hustle and bustle of everyday people.

Theseweredoneinthehopethat Iwouldfeelaliveandbecomefree from the thoughts of Mother. Sometimes, wandering in the street would make me desire to speak to someone. At other times, I just wanted to observe men of the world, what they radiate to the world as well as the plethora of emotions they evoked and felt.

I felt that some people had a certain level of satisfaction and purpose, which made me feel miserable, as I have not found that which was truly meant for me despite the fortune I had. One that looked utterly perfect, that seemed to have found his or her purpose, would still die just like Father and Aunt Suzzy died despite how much hope doctors dangled before us.

I had fortune and was ready to believe in the tiniest grain of hope that Mother would quickly recover. I was willing to lay down all my fortune, if given the chance to, so that Mother would live. I must feel the pain of those I was better than, those that couldn't have my fortune, despite making endless sacrifices. There were those who found a level of contentment in their poverty or whatever level they found themselves in. The thought of using my fortunes to buy life will vanish, for we all shall die. The worst that one can do was not knowing how to live.

I have invented a life of competition, in which I seek to acquire more and move faster, but I shall slow down because I have to live. It was hard to find one who is content with what they have. Despite having 99 sheep, Master still desired to have the 1 that was missing. If Master wasn't content with having 99 sheep, how could I be content with what I had? Many who claimed to be content would secretly desire things not belonging to them, while concealing it from others. If what they desired was given to them, they will surely accept it rather than reject it.

Mother wasn't getting better. The thought of being with her while she didn't get better made me sad. I sought to leave her

presence. I desired the presence of Ella. Ella was busy and said to me politely, 'Please sit here, I will be back soon.' I obeyed and, for hours, I sat rooted to the spot. I kept watching her as she carried trays of different items without saying a word to me. I believe she enjoyed her work. I think that she found her true purpose in helping people and saving lives. I desired to talk to her only because I felt peace on hearing her voice.

After waiting for a while, I decided to leave and swore not to talk to her; to turn my back on her even if she ever talked to me. However, after a moment, these thoughts vanished, and I desired to talk to her again. She had less time for me, as her desire had always been to help people. I believed that Master must have given her some power with which to care for people, just like Master would give different people temporary powers to lead, to teach, to take life, to steal and do so much more.

In times when Ella acted like I never existed, I wandered back to the streets to avoid going to the presence of Mother. We were closer now but the very thought of losing Mother made me find a way to be free of the pain it would cause me.

I had a premonition when I was out on the streets. It was confirmed when I returned to the hospital. Ella was at the front door. She looked swollen and dull, which was not typical of her. She asked where I had been, noting that she had searched for me. Why would someone search for another person that they had neglected?

By the look on her face, I could tell that something wasn't right. The thought of Mother rang instantly, in my head. Ella didn't have to say the words; I could read them all over her. I wanted, more than anything, not to believe the words she had said to me.

She hugged me tightly; this was the first time she ever hugged me. I truly needed it as I cried uncontrollably on her shoulders. I had not cried like this, for most of my life.

My deepest fear had become a reality. I cried out; ruining some peaceful moments of others in the world. I had truly felt the pain that others felt, which made them cry out late at night and I sought to chastise them for ruining my perfect moment. I didn't even feel this pain when Father had died. I could now say that the world has taken something, something that I felt belonged to me, from me.

How long, before this emotion finally overwhelms me? How long, till damnation catches up with my poor soul? How long, before I break down like others before me, who suffered losses that couldn't be recovered? How long, before my end starts coming and I was forced again to find ways to live, with the little time I have left?

I must shut down many of my fears, so as to find ways to survive in the painful world of humans. I would bring my repressed desires and deeds to the surface; repressed desires of being a coward, a weakling or fragile. Ella was comforting me, at this point. I knew I was now alone in the world but I didn't care what anyone thought of me; whether as a weakling, a coward or

fragile. It dawned on me how strong I have been in times past, but not now.

I had shown strength and bravery, by my ability to protect myself from the exploitation of those that intended to drown me in their expectations and desires. I had unknowingly carried out the expectations of others rather than mine. It felt right that I'm a weakling in the world. I should probably be dead, as Mother was.

I had become lost, just like many in the world that lost themselves after losing something that was precious to them. I was lost in the presence of Ella, with no peace coming from it any more. I was lost in thought. What could be more painful than death, than losing a loved one? How could I recover?

If one loses a fortune, one may work hard again to re-acquire it. If one is heartbroken, one will seek to find another to love. If one loses a leg, one may seek a prosthesis. If a woman loses a child, the woman may be pregnant again. She could heal from her pain and transfer more love to the world as well as to the new baby (if she gets one).

What shall I do? Tell me, what shall I do, now that I have lost a mother? Should I find a way to bring her back to life? That could happen only in my head, where she should live rent free. Could I call another person my mother? I doubted it.

People always tend to speak well of the dead, no matter how badly they lived. When a person who has spent his or her lifetime doing wrong dies, some people will still speak good of him or her.

Why do people tend to speak good of a completely evil person? Perhaps, their evil deeds weren't extended to or seen by everyone. If one gains something from an evil person, then the evil one will become good to the one who has gained from him or her.

I must tell you, you must only speak good about Mother for she had done only good to me, to you and to the world in the little way she can. The death of Father wasn't like the death of Mother, in terms of its effects on me. I experienced pain when Father died, but it was not as much as that which I felt when Mother died.

How long will I remain in this abyss that I dare not call life? How can I escape it? If I would desire and draw a conclusion to take my life, I would still leave behind a cycle of pain. This was a cycle in which the world has been stuck, from the beginning of time when Master pursued man out of the garden and cursed mankind in anger.

I must again question Master's decision to rid me of the things I loved the most, in a short span of time. However, I shall find ways to heal from the pain I felt, so as to give the world a chance to heal.

Chapter Sixteen

In the human world, fortune favours the bold; those willing to take risks. What is the need of having knowledge if it can not be expressed in various forms so as to bring men to your side? On the path to damnation shall men swiftly find themselves, for not expressing their knowledge in various forms and not bringing men to their side with their knowledge.

We need to express ourselves, to console and be consoled, to understand and be understood, to love and be loved. I experienced a void left by something; I was in a world that felt empty without Mother in it. I had the need to be accepted, despite having claimed that I desired not the acceptance of men because of the fortunes I had. Deep in those underlying thoughts of mine, I did not desire the acceptance of all men but the acceptance of

Ella alone. I needed Ella to accept and understand me, to love me so I could love her, for she was all I desired.

I desired to evoke feelings in Ella even though I couldn't tell whether or not she loved me. There would be no hospital visits again, not of my making, but because Mother had died and there won't be an opportunity in the nearest future to see Ella again. If the hospital couldn't heal Mother but many received their healing at the hospital, then I must believe that the hospital was not a place that could heal everyone. It was sometimes a place of passage to a new world, either to damnation or to heavenly paradise.

Ella's understanding of me and love for me were what I desired of her. Was she pretending? Did she understand me but chose to show little or no emotions towards me? Was I hoping to find a feeling of satisfaction in the fact that someone would finally be able to understand and love me? Was this all I truly needed?

This feeling I had towards Ella, was it real? Whenever we talked on the phone, I couldn't bring myself to hang up. She had become my daily obsession. This was unlike my experience with any other lady I had met, in times past. I wanted to be in her presence always, to love her, to hold her hands, to look into her eyes and find peace within my troubled soul.

I must ask questions about Ella who worked in the hospital where countless deaths had occurred and would still occur. Were her feelings genuine or had they been numbed by the endless number of deaths she had witnessed? The mere sight of

a dying being is likely to trigger certain pain in a living person; this pain was perhaps for the dead person or for the wailing that will surely follow the death of a person.

It seemed it had become a tradition that, when someone had died, people came to pay their condolences. This always irked me. Men's desire to connect with other beings, their claim that they feel the pain of the bereaved and their desire to be there for someone who has lost someone or something was part of the reasons of condolence visit.

The several good things that were said about Mother made me wonder whether she was truly free of flaws while she was alive. It was not that I wanted to hear the bad aspects of Mother but the fact is that she was human and was bound to have flaws. A perfect woman she was; that was what most people, who called me or came to visit me, said. I was surprised when people called her perfect. How about the lies she told to help me? One would call that love and sacrifice but did lying not take away from the saying that Mother was perfect?

I had opened myself and my corner to the world of men. This was not because I wanted to but because I felt I had no choice, My corner was busy with the coming and going of creatures that I had despised for long; creatures I rarely desired. I desired Ella but she would never come. 'I'll make out time,' she always said to me. She was always working.

My cousin stayed with me for a while, to keep me company and to console me. Paul had come and gone. Sophia did come, much to my surprise. 'I desired to see you, to know how you are,' she said to me. She said many encouraging words to me. It dawned on me that Sophia no longer evoked emotions in me like she did in times past. I felt happy seeing Sophia. However, thoughts of Ella and the torment of losing my parents were at the forefront of my mind. Nothing else mattered.

There were several people who were coming to and going from my corner, as well as so many calls; but none did I desire like Ella. My corner, once a solitary place and my place of solace, has now been fully opened to others. I feared that, if people ventured into my corner for long, they would become me. Also, I realised that the more people ventured into my corner, the more I became like them.

I had become like those who ventured into my corner and started taking various forms, depending on who visited me. With one who came crying, I cried; by one who came comforting, I was comforted. With one who come singing, I sang. With one who came laughing, I laughed.

I was no longer myself, for the more people I came in contact with, the more I took up a part of them. I must believe that they took a part of me but I couldn't tell for sure. I have finally become of the world. It was whatever they desired me to be that I shall be. I was letting myself get stuck with the desires of the world; after all, I couldn't claim to be wise, to be perfect or to have knowledge if these didn't have a corresponding influence on people. I couldn't claim to be me if I became whatever people desired me to be.

I needed to have my own shape and form. I should be wiser, and yet never claim to be perfect or more knowledgeable, than others. This is because, at some point, someone greater would appear; for those who claim to possess a wealth of knowledge aren't always wise because even their knowledge won`t always save them.

At random times, I sought to flee my corner to find solace elsewhere. Miriam wanted to follow me everywhere but I always found a way for that not to happen. I could sense that her persistence to follow me everywhere was out of love and care for me. I would drive to the road, where I knew the thought of Ella would arise; as it always happened. She had been the one I endlessly yearned for and I desired to see her quickly. She would be at the hospital; a place I had despised and vowed to never go again. Suddenly, I began to contemplate going to a place I despised, just to see one I desired.

I arrived the hospital where Ella welcomed me with open arms, which was not typical of her. We would sit; looking at each other. There and then, the thought of Mother would quickly arise to haunt me. This made my mind go blank and I would have no idea what to say to Ella. Oh, what pain could do to someone!

The promises I made previously, to be better, would rise to the surface as well. I could not keep my promise to Mother, to Master who resides above, to people whom I find myself with or to myself. On the path to damnation I shall find myself for failing to keep my promises to Master, to men and even to myself. My word was worthless to anyone I gave it, because I struggled to be sure of who I was, as I took various forms in the world. We all do, sometimes.

The promises I made to heal myself in the world and to find peace in the presence of Ella were bound to be broken. Suddenly, the desire to be in the presence of Ella would vanish and I would seek to leave her presence. I would think about some of Master's promises, in times past, that have failed to become reality especially since affliction that wasn't meant to rise the second time did rise. How else could I explain losing Mother after losing Father? Master failed to keep His promises; how could I keep mine? Why would He let me lose Mother after losing Father?

I began to tell Ella that the patients needed her. She told me she was on a break, and I wondered whether she was keeping people's lives on hold. This was even though I knew that there was someone else doing her job, at the moment. I sought a way to flee her presence without sowing confusion, doubt or strife into her mind like I did to Sophia. I felt that I loved Ella and wouldn't want to hurt one I did love.

All of a sudden, another nurse ran to us to tell Ella that she was being called. 'It's an emergency,' she said and I would feel a certain burden being lifted off me. Ella rose; promising to come see me in the evening. I would quickly stutter a response and watch her beautiful well-sculpted body as she left my presence.

I drove back to my corner; expecting her. I desired a perfect end to the day, which was when Ella would come visit me. At first, when I got back to my corner, I would be filled with happiness, happiness

I rarely felt in times past. Swiftly, just as it came, the happiness would give way to doubt about whether I was truly deserving of love. I had questions about Ella's decision to visit me. Was it out of sympathy for me who had lost Mother? Was it because she truly loved me or because of my daily insistence on seeing her?

I felt I was forcing myself on her but Ella acted like she didn't care about anything relating to me. Whenever we talked or I visited her at the hospital, I tried to express my emotions so as to make her show some feelings of love or care for me. She displayed apathy instead and sometimes, I sought to annoy her. When she got angry, any sense of tranquillity that existed in my mind would vanish; owing to my decisions to annoy Ella. I felt that Ella was like Father; one that rarely showed any emotions yet truly cared.

Ella arrived at my corner by some minutes past 6 in the evening, to my surprise. My cousin, Miriam, who stayed with me had gone to visit to a friend. She would return in a day or two. Ella arrived, looking more beautiful than I thought, for she was not wearing scrubs. In the first few minutes of her arrival, I just sat; looking and smiling at her. This made her uncomfortable. Truly, she had become my happiness.

Ella stood and walked around my house. I kept looking at how beautiful this creature was. 'Her soul must be in perfect order,' I thought. It would dawn on me that there was a pattern that kept recurring, in my life and in the world we live. Sophia made me uncomfortable and here I was, making Ella uncomfortable. In both situations, love was present but not reciprocated.

I must come to believe that one couldn't exist in life without cycles and patterns; which showed in various ways. There wasa time to crawl, a time to walk, a time to live, a time to die and so many others. One that did walk could go back to crawling and walking, again. There were no schedules for the cycles of life. I must bring myself to the present, to enjoy the presence of Ella whom I endlessly desired. She was right in front of me asI fixated my eyes to her, just like Master fixated His eyes on theworld.

Ella gushed over how arranged my corner was. It wasn't me; it was Miriam's handiwork. However, I needed to put up the appearance of a gentleman or a principled man. If my mind was filled with the disorder and anguish of my daily life, is it right that my corner be disarranged? If I allow the disorders of my daily life and mind to seep out, I shall find myself on the path of damnation for setting a path of destruction for the world; with my various thoughts and desires that they shall come to know of.

Ella sat close to me and asked more questions about my life. I was not necessarily comfortable with that, but I must answer her if I was to win a place in her heart. I knew within me that I wasn't a principled man. I had sometimes disobeyed rules and done whatever I desired, which was not always my fault. However, at this time, I sought to please Ella and win her over.

'What about your friends?' she asked, out of surprise that no one came to visit me.

'I need no friends,' I said to her.

My fortune brought many friends and lovers to me, none of which I desired. I had lied to her, just like I lied for the most part of my life; just like many in the world did lie even when it was not necessary. I lied when I said I needed no friends and lovers, for I feared for myself and for love. I was afraid of someone else knowing who I was, what I looked like deep inside and what I desired.

Even now when I answered Ella's question, some answers were truths laced with lies. After all, without lies, some beings in the world would never move forward. So, I must believe that, if the truth will always set you free, then lying will sometimes set you free. If lying was bound to get you locked up, then even the truth would sometimes get you locked up. On the path to damnation we shall find ourselves, for lying and seeking to mislead others, to our advantage.

I doubted if Ella truly loved me. I had doubts because of the way she talked. How could she be pessimistic and call her herself a healer, a nurse? She said to me, 'I have seen death, countless times. Would love keep one alive a little longer? Would love save us all? If bad things filled the world, shouldn't one prepare for such things?' All of these, and more, she said when I confessed my love to her. I wondered how one could sit and prepare; waiting for bad to happen.

Ella was someone who was filled with endless knowledge, which she sought to repress just as she did with her emotions. She didn't want anyone to know how smart she was. She spoke like one who believed in nothing; like one that did what she felt was necessary, in the world, till the end would come. She talked like one whose desires were not of this world.

I thought to myself that, perhaps, her environment did change her. I wasn't entirely sure if she was morphed into something better or worse, as she didn't give me any form of access to her mind. What if, in a bid to heal others, the healer was getting sick and couldn't tell that she was sick? If the healer would heal plenty of men and failed to heal herself, what shall one say? Shall we truly call her a healer?

What if Master, in a bid to save the world, couldn't save everyone? Shall we call Master the saviour of us all if He can`t save everyone? If one who had sand in his eyes sought to remove the sand in his brother's eyes, while neglecting to remove the sand in his eyes, was that love or hypocrisy? Did Master approve of that? Would such a person be deserving of Master's love, for his sacrifice to another? We couldn't tell as one couldn't fully understand the mystic ways of the world. Due to all the questions one asked and got no answer, one should begin to lose faith in Master or in any supernatural higher beings. On the path to damnation I shall find myself, for failing to trust in Master who led men in time past with cloud by day and fire by night. Those days would rarely come again as men currently misled their fellow men for their own gain.

Should we desire days past when Master's fury did reign - destroying at will those that showed a little sign of evil - and when humans did eat angels' food? Not again, as Master's fury has given way to love for humans like me; seen in the many chances He gives us. It will be a long time to come before humans would eat food sent from heaven again, as the hungry will surely starve to death if they did not work or steal. If one doesn't work or steal, then one is bound to die. Perhaps, one can desire to give food freely, but it will not always be so.

Ella would say that a person lives because that was Master's will and that one recovers because it was destined that they recover. If one spent a lifetime praying for food or whatever he or she desired, then one lives a lifetime expecting food or whatever they desired. However, sometimes, those things elude one.

I was concerned about Ella. She possessed a wealth of knowledge and was too secure in it. No matter how much I tried, I couldn't work my way to her mind to gather more information. I felt that I became what I was, mostly because of the world and immediate environment I have found myself in.

If my environment was filled with war, then I believed that the world is a place of war. If my environment was filled with pain, I tended to believe the world is filled with pain. If I lived and grew up in poverty, I expected that the world was filled with poverty. The environment people find themselves in plays a major role in shaping what they become and believe about the world. However, we have to grow and learn from wherever we find ourselves, to get better and find something better.

Our minds must not remain static in whatever situation we find ourselves. We must seek something better than what we find ourselves in. I must seek to find peace if I was in a war-filled place. I must seek abundance of fortune if I found myself in poverty. I must seek something other than that which I was stuck in. The world must desire to let me grow. I must desire to grow; to imbibe better knowledge, connection and thought pattern; to seek and believe in a higher version of me.

However, Ella won't do these, as she couldn't change. 'You can't change all the pain, heartbreak and trauma that someone has experienced,' she said to me. 'It has become a part of them.' She would never explain in detail what happened to her in times past.

it was our choice to look at the world and see differently from what the reality was. I despised myself and others for causing pain to many in the world. I thought of the connection of Josephine and Sophia; of all the anguish I bore towards them. However, if I bore anguish towards them, how can I know whether they bore anguish towards me and repressed it; not just from me but from the world?

Ella would decline to spend the night at my corner. I drove her home while thinking about another moment I would spend in her presence.

I struggled to sleep, that night. I remembered vividly when Paul would cry about a lady he loved. He had spoken to me endlessly of her beauty. I found myself laughing, wondering what could make a man cry over a creature of the opposite sex. I may experience the same thing in the long run, since I had made Ella the architect of my happiness.

I believed I would cry out my soul if she ever stopped designing my happiness. How foolish I was, to make another being the source of my happiness! I must find happiness from within myself, even though I knew I did a perfect job at lying to myself; just as many in the world did.

I had once said to myself that nobody could hurt me without my permission but I was wrong. Who could give another the permission to hurt him or her? Why would I desire that someone hurt me? I realised that, by loving someone, you give them the permission to hurt you. By Master's love for us, He had given us permissions to hurt Him endlessly and in love, He forgives us the same way we forgive those we love.

Ella was hurting me without my permission. She did it so perfectly that I would always revere her for all the pain she caused me and all the mixed signals she threw at me. I sought to understand why I desired to love and have one that caused me pain. Man's desire, sometimes, is to be with the little known rather than the full unknown.

I would imagine one being in hell and then declining opportunities to finally make it to heaven. This may be because of a certain satisfaction in being in hell or the falsehood that, if one lived long in hell, it may finally become heaven to them. How could one believe in heaven if they found a certain level of satisfaction in hell? I may come to believe that heaven could become hell and hell could, one day, become heaven.

Whatafalseideologythatwillcontinuetocloudman'sjudgement!

People like Ella, who had vast knowledge, existed. They must have accumulated knowledge over the years they have spent living in the world, or received it from above. Yet, there were many who desired knowledge and wisdom; both of which kept eluding them.

Thus, I questioned the source of the knowledge that I used to write this. Was this knowledge from above or accumulated from the world, which made me begin to feel I was better than many in the world? Would knowledge from above or accumulated knowledge from the world save us all? I couldn't tell.

If many can't hear Master vividly, how can they claim to have knowledge from Him? Did our minds and intuition rise to a level where they spoke to us, like a voice from outside us; a voice that told us about things that we never knew about? Was it the voice of Master?

If I believed I was born into the world with a blank state and I filed my mind - with my experience, my ideas, my surroundings and my thoughts and so much more, some which was not of my making -then I should believe that there is no such thing as accumulated knowledge or knowledge from above. All that you know is all that you are.

If, in my few years on earth, I would dare not say that I have seen everything that the world has to offer, how can another who has lived for 80 years claim to have seen all that the world has to offer? I wouldn't believe such, as one can not see all that the world has to offer. I came to believe that, in my few years on earth, I saw what I was bound to see.

No one can claim to have seen all that the world has to offer. You only see what you decide to see or what you are shown. That partly explains why one born in extreme poverty will tend to believe that the entire world is in poverty and that he is bound to be poor. Perhaps, his mind limits him. If, after endless attempts to escape poverty, poverty never eludes him, shall others in the world not grow their fortune because one believed that the world is in poverty?

People find themselves in various situations that they believe were meant to be for them, as they couldn't see an escape route or a shining light to guide or save them. As a result of their mindsets, many have accepted their fate and they no longer take the initiative to change it. On the path of damnation we shall find ourselves, for not desiring self-development which will surely result in the development of the world.

What shall I say, if Ella would force me to think deeply about the very existence of myself? The very source of my knowledge intertwined with my very desire to be loved by her. If I find myself on the wrong side of life by crying over a female, what then shall I call myself? Shall I call myself a weakling for crying over Mother or crying over Ella? The world will decide what I shall be called. Some would call me strong while others would call me weak. Does it really matter? Well, not to me. One would do only good and be called bad; another could do only bad and be called good.

Was I not allowed to cry? Am I not a human? Was it wrong to cry over a woman? Well, I forced myself to cry, just to please people, in times past. If I cried over Mother and found myself at some point crying over Ella, then I would be happy to. This was because those cries came from my heart and flowed naturally. Thus, it was up to men in the world to either accept me or look at me in whatever way they desired. To each, his own opinion; as I felt I would be better and grow in the world if I had Ella's love all to myself.

I woke from sleep, feeling heavy. Fear clouded my mind. What have I done! It would dawn on me that the bold will swiftly be condemned to damnation, as the swiftness of their actions would leave no room for correction, in the long run. I realised that my timidity and introversion had saved me, most times in the world, but not any longer.

Now that I was bold and had decided to open myself to the world as well as to Ella, what shall they find out? In a bid to be loved by Ella, what have I said to her? Both the timid as well as the bold that lacked self-control and discipline, will be swiftly condemned to eternal damnation.

Chapter Seventeen

I would like to know the thoughts that men had against me but I can't. Knowing the full thoughts of humans will remain elusive, to not just me but also to all humans who desired to know the thoughts of other humans. People were good at hiding their emotions, desires and thoughts. With varying amounts of information shown by one to another, one could know, to a little extent, the desires and thoughts of another man. What about the thoughts I imagine towards others?

In times past when my thoughts would seek to torment me, I would make haste to take actions by twisting my mind to believe I had done right; instead of accepting the wrong and evil I had done. It would dawn on me that I was not deserving of the love of people and especially not that of Ella. I deserved only the hatred of men, for, in a bid to win Ella's heart, I had poured out my deepest and repressed secrets to her. I told her that I did kill Aunt Suzzy. I cried out to Ella about the mistakes I had made. I found a way to lie to myself so as to repress and hide my deeds, not just from men of the world but from myself as well.

My real self was a killer. I left home in times past to live with Aunt Suzzy, hoping to find freedom. However, her incessant shouting and questions about my future made me desire that grievous things happen to her. This was even though she only wanted me to learn, grow and be better. My accumulation of evil desires will burst one day and find itself out of control. I let the daily disorder of my mind seep out into reality. I recalled doing some research so I could find ways to kill myself, owing to my failures in the world.

I intended to find ways to escape the world of pain I found myself in. I was so bent on this that, in a swift change of heart, I began to have thoughts of killing another being. It was not just anyone but my aunt under whose roof I stayed. She cared for me as she sought to mould me into a better being, so I could conquer the world and find my true self.

Oh, how the human heart can never be fully satisfied! Oh, how the vast resources available to men will be abused by them! The information readily available in the internet gave me various painless ways to kill oneself, one of which was ingesting a chemical. I could no longer remember the name of the chemical when I told Ella, for my endless desire now was Ella; her love was all I desired and her love would be the end of me. I bought the chemical.

Aunt Suzzy returned from a long journey, quite weak. Despite the many workers and housekeepers that she had, she had screamed that I get her a glass of water. I was so shaken that I swiftly put the colourless chemical, which was close by, into the water I gave to her.

She drank it and complained that it had an unusual taste. She told me to make sure that the water supply system was cleaned the next day, I nodded. Feelings of guilt mixed with those of happiness were what I felt. At some point, after her death, I was angry with myself for causing pain to Miriam and to others who loved my aunt.

The morning after Aunt Suzzy's death was confirmed, I was particularly bold. I did not act in accordance with the timidity and shyness attributed to me. I cried loudly and sought to comfort Miriam. I was surprised at my actions, but I knew I needed to keep up with them so as to avoid suspicion. Could anyone be blamed for not suspecting me? No one could ever suspect me as being behind the death of Aunt Suzzy, for no one ever imagined that Aunt Suzzy was killed.

It was said that she died of natural causes because no autopsy was carried out on the corpse. If this happened in a more developed country, someone would be curious enough to ask for the autopsy report. In this part of the world, people believed that vengeance was to be left for Master. Also, modern religion - which people have currently accepted - forbade the use of traditional diviners in such a matter. No one was to talk about the dead, for they should let the dead be dead. Afterwards, plans for her funeral were made.

Following the death of Aunt Suzzy, I had been rather close and far to Miriam whom I had made an orphan by killing her mother. An orphan I was now, as the cycle will come back to haunt me. I must seek to understand whether I was destined to kill Aunt Suzzy, for, if I haven't killed her, I wouldn't have received the fortune willed to me. I wouldn't have found myself in my corner, as I used the fortune to buy myself a house; for I couldn't be here without this fortune.

I had a feeling that I had a higher purpose than others. After the birth of Master, many children were killed so that Master would live. If children were sacrificed so Master would live and fulfil His purpose of dying for our sins as well as bringing salvation to mankind, then I must believe that Aunt Suzzy was sacrificed so I could go higher and have this fortune.

The children, whom I felt were without sin, were bound to die so that Master could rise. I was bound and destined to kill Aunt Suzzy so I could rise higher and have this fortune, for if Aunt Suzzy hadn't died, then I would have been somewhere not typical of where I was now. I would be in a place where many would neither desire to know me nor even hear of me. I may have been forgotten.

I couldn't know whether I would have had fortunes in time to come without killing Aunt Suzzy. I wouldn't know because the decisions I made then by killing Aunt Suzzy altered my future (current outcome). I had no expectations or desires of fortune when I killed my aunt. I killed her, out of spite, for always troubling me but the decision I made to kill Aunt Suzzy was enough to get me to this very moment where I had fortunes to myself.

My present was filled with anguish and uncertainty. It will cost me my life in time to come; this I believed, for I had killed a creature that Master made. On the path to damnation I shall find myself, for killing one created by Master and causing pain to the beings of the world.

I wondered if Aunt Suzzy's good deeds might land her in heavenly paradise. I couldn't tell where she was, as I was not given the opportunity to know. I wondered if she made it to heavenly paradise and watched, from above, the evil I had done by killing her, despite the good thoughts she had for me.

Did she feel pain or joy, when she saw this? What would Master say to her? 'Your good deeds brought you here?' or 'You were bound to die by someone close to you, by one whom you love?' Was it a series of unfortunate events that led to her death? I asked this question, for if I had achieved all my desires without fail, I would have neither had thoughts to kill myself nor bought the chemical I discovered on the internet. This chemical was intended to kill me but I had used it to kill Aunt Suzzy. Was she still angry with me, from above or below? I couldn't know.

I hid my feelings, actions and thoughts from myself until my love for Ella brought them to the surface. My desire to love was making me open myself up to Ella. No one could play the game of hiding his or her emotions better than a guilty person. I was quick to realise that the source of my restlessness so far, despite my fortune, was the accumulation of the evil I had done in the world. It was the pain I had caused to humans.

Once I hurt someone else, the thought that I had killed Aunt Suzzy would slowly seep out and I would repress it. This would make me start to find ways to please, or forget, the one I hurt before I would develop a desire to kill the person.

Maybe my mind, which was the very source of the evil, would be the very thing saving me and bringing me to redemption rather than drawing me closer to damnation. If my mind, which was the source of all the evil I had caused so far in life, could save me and still end me, I must come to feel that I wasn't the creator or architect of my mind. I was never in control. I did whatever it desired or whatever others desired of it; a fool I was.

Why did I tell the truth in the evil world of men; for redemption or condemnation? I've known, in the course of my life, that telling the truth doesn't always set a man free, even though Master had said that the truth will set you free.

My telling the truth to Ella would mean a lot of things. These include Miriam hating me forever, for taking the life of her precious mother, my aunt. Also, it utterly meant I should hate Master and the spirit of death for taking my precious parents from me. It signified that the police would seek to apprehend me and I would escape. It would mean that those that loved me, as well as Ella whom I had opened myself to in the hope that she will love me, would forget me because of my evil acts.

Just like the bad, the good shall soon be forgotten.

Why would speaking the truth signify a sudden bondage to myself as well as to the world, and lying keep me sane? Now that I had spoken the truth, men shall desire to take my freedom away from me. Why did I decide to say the truth to Ella? It was too late for that question and for regrets.

I had told all to Ella. Her confidence was unmatched as she did not show any signs of fear that I was a killer. I drove her home and still expected to be in her presence again, despite having told her the evil I had done. She smiled and talked as I drove to her house.

Would Ella suddenly say all I told her, to the world? It dawned on me that I was insane to trust that Ella won't tell the world what I have done. Ella was the end of me; love was the end of me. I decided unintentionally, not to have my freedom, by speaking the truth. Tell me, was it right that I have my freedom as well as the endless torment of my soul if I hadn't spoken the truth to Ella, one whom I loved? I told the truth and I was no longer free. Thus, I confirmed my fears that speaking the truth won't always set free.

Is life worth more than dying, for in dying are we born to eternal life? Not everyone is born to eternal life; some, like me, are bound to eternal damnation. If I must go down to the grave and believe I would come up no more to heavenly paradise, why then shall I desire to go down to the grave without the very least of my freedom? I must hold on to my freedom in the world, as I became sure that my desire of ascending to heavenly paradise was no more.

I would have hidden myself and the truth if I wasn't sure of heavenly paradise. Now, it was late. I had no more freedom in the world and I shall go down to the grave that way. I believe that Master would punish me for my sins in the world.

I must also believe that Master, being one who has mercy and compassion, may decide not to punish my poor soul for my sins and I shall find myself on the path to heavenly paradise. What then shall I say? Filled with joy, I should have sinned far more than I did initially. In more damnation I shall find myself, for despite having hopes to be saved, I still desired more things of the world.

He who strives to save his life shall lose it but he who loses his life for Master's sake shall gain it. I desired saving, but with all the evil I had done, I had known for a long time that nothing could fill me up to make me feel perfect and whole in the world; not even my fortune, my love for Ella or the endless desire to be accepted by people. I speak for myself, as many in the world of men should speak for themselves. I desired to have many things, in a bid to feel whole and perfect.

People differ in their desires and in their search for what will make them whole. Love makes some whole. Finding a purpose makes others whole. Fortune makes another set of people whole and so many other things exist that would make people whole in the world. The hearts of men differ in their desires. How swiftly things change in the world, for something that made you whole could at some point make you feel empty!

Why was it that, it was when many desired freedom and peace from the sudden death of Aunt Suzzy, that I sought to bring back the past and open up old wounds? I truly loved Ella and I felt I did not deserve her. Could I lie to the one I love? I felt that my mind was troubled and only Ella's love could calm it. My desire for Ella caused me to speak the truth to her about what I had done. I told her my sins so she could love me more. I wanted her to know the whole, undiluted and hidden version of me. Oh, how love would be the end of us! If only Ella would accept me and what I have done, it would bring out the best in me!

How could it be, despite the years I had spent living in the world, that I felt that Ella's love would bring out the best in me? How did I imagine that Ella would accept me after everything I told her? Show me one who is without sin among people. I committed murder, which is a sin against Master, but I felt that one who has spent a lifetime killing people would have his or her reasons that made him or her to believe that murder was not a sin. Another who has spent a lifetime lying would do the same as well, all for various reasons and satisfactions.

Many had committed many grievous sins which they sought to mask, in a bid to conquer the world and find their ways to the top. Must I come to believe that it was a good thing that I had killed Aunt Suzzy, as I was on the top now? On the path to damnation we shall find ourselves, for seeking to make bad things look good.

By striving to save my life, to find love, freedom and so many things, I was losing them even though I knew my life never belonged to me.

Oh, tell me how a creature could make another better! If Ella was leading me to damnation, how could I say she was making me better? I must say that Ella has power, astonishing power, over me. I had opened myself, my deepest secret, to her. It made me scared of what I may become, now that Ella knew all about me.

Now that another being has finally been given access to my soul, to my mind, it dawned on me that I barely had control over the events of my life and my thoughts. The death of Mother must have happened so I could get close to Ella, so that someone could have access to my mind.

How foolish I was, to believe that the sudden increase in my sufferings would bring about a higher chance of redemption to my poor soul! After all, I felt I barely had full control over the events in my life.

If I did all the evil I recalled, then it feels right that I was a nightmare or an eyesore to the world; due to all my evil acts. Underneath these thoughts, I believed that I caused

my failings. It was not Master, not my surroundings, not anybody else or the world. I was the cause of it all. If at this moment, I was failing to be sure of myself, what then shall I do? Shall I rid myself of myself?

What shall I become if, due to my outpouring of truth to Ella, she couldn't love me any more? Shall I seek to rid the world of Ella as well? What shall I become, if Master fails to accept me? On the path to damnation I shall find myself then.

What shall I say when Ella asks who she is to me? What shall I reply when she says I could kill her too? Oh dear, can I ask myself whom I wasn't sure of, what we've done with this life we found ourselves in? Can I ask myself who we are? I filled myself with pain for my failures, with hope and promises that I couldn't keep. The pain was stronger and more controlling than the hope and promises.

I had desires, just like others; which included an elusive desire for heavenly paradise. Most people desired heavenly paradise but aren't worthy of it; they weren't ready to work towards it. This was a world of elusive hope, the coming which Master foretold and in which He expected men of the world to be at the forefront of dominion. However, men can't dominate; for many people had vicious desires concealed within themselves and one will never know the true intentions of one human to another.

I might have told the truth to Ella when I confessed to killing Aunt Suzzy, out of love and in confidence, but I will have to take it back. I sought immediately to take back my words, seeking to let her know it was all a lie. I told the truth mistakenly with the very acceptance of me by Ella in my mind, but I can no longer agree on the truth as Ella left me. This forced me to take back the truth I had spoken out but it would be to no avail, as Ella took my truth into the world and the world had accepted it. This was a truth I had told her out of love and in confidence; now, I have to fight this battle all by myself.

Perhaps there's a battle for everyone; there must always be an enemy for one to conquer. However, if one who has everyone on his side desired an enemy, then he must surely make an enemy from one who's on his side.

I had cut myself off from the world but what shall I gain? I knew that, as Ella took the truth into the world, people will seek to make me an enemy. They will find me mentally and physically repulsive, because I killed another person. I felt I was ready to live with that, only if Ella would accept me.

I felt I could overcome this moment if Ella would accept and love me, but she wouldn't. I desired to be accepted by Ella and not the world I lived in. How could I not be accepted by humans? Again, would Master claim to be Master if He wasn't accepted by the world He found himself in? How could He call Himself the saviour of the world if He couldn't save everyone?

I couldn't view myself as an entity outside the world but as one that needs to change. I must seek to view myself as an entity inside the world. It was a world in which my decisions had a corresponding effect on others. I feel broken, owing to the wrong decisions I made, as I could no longer change the world. On the path of damnation I shall find myself, for desiring to change the world without desiring to change myself.

By cutting myself off from the world, I had hidden myself from the world; hiding from the sins I had committed yet having a certain belief that I could be saved and that Master's redemption could be mine. I must decide to raise my hope and grow my survival chances, having hidden far away from everyone in another house with the desire for a fresh start and to escape all those that desired to hurt me. This was because Ella had told the world what I had done and the world sough to apprehend me. I would seek to evade and forget everything about my past life.

My phone rang. Sophia was the caller. It would dawn on me that, despite my desire to forget my past life, I desired elements of it. What did Sophia want? To mock or to comfort me? I ignored the call and broke the phone.

How could I desire a fresh start and still hang on to things from the past? I must tell you, there would be no safe haven for me in the world. I desired, for one last time, to understand the workings of the world and the very purpose of my existence.

Am I free? Are we really free?

He who is without sin should cast the first stone and I believe that many counted me worthy of death, because they felt that my sin of murder covers all their sins. Shall I blame them? Will they, all of a sudden believe themselves to be without sin, to be without flaws? I must tell you, we deceive and lie to ourselves if we claim to be without sin.

Did someone whisper into my ears the ideas that I felt belonged to me? Perhaps, someone else was in control of my mind. Everything I knew, I believed Master wanted me to know. There was no knowledge bestowed on me or that I accumulated without the consent of Master. The knowledge of either good or evil came from Master. So, if I had killed, then Master desired for me to kill. If I lied, then Master desired for me to lie and so on. A fool I was, for how could I believe that Master was the voice telling me good as well as bad?

Most times, I couldn't say no to what the voice desired. In this moment, in my most conscious self, I could see that the voice brought me closer to damnation. The voice that was a close companiontomeintimespast, thatmadesomedecisionswithout my consent and sough to control me, was it really Master? On the path to damnation I shall find myself, for failing to discern between the voices which were of Master and those which weren't.

If my mind was the greatest weapon that could make or destroy me, why then was it that I remained conscious and sane, sometimes free of anguish caused by murder? I had lived my life so far like I hadn't done something horrible. Perhaps, my mind was indeed my saviour as it saved me in times past from the torment of what I have done.

I wondered how I could have still lived without hiding if I hadn't met Ella. Remember when I said she was from Master and I believed she had been sent to expose me. Of course, in due time, many will be sent to expose the wickedness of other men. I gladly desire the exposure of the wickedness of others, so as to find a moment's peace for myself, knowing that I won't be alone on the path to damnation.

Even as I hid from the world, in my new corner, I desired to know what happened outside. I heard of how Paul was slowly rising to the top of the ladder of success. I no longer desired the good things of the world for myself or Mother who was no longer in the world but for my friends and loved ones. These included: Miriam, Paul, Josephine, Ella, Sophia and all those who showed me love indeed.

I felt that desiring good for others, who had done evil in times past, would set me on the path to redemption. However, I knew that Master would forgive all who ask for forgiveness for their sinful ways. These included Paul who stole in times past when he did have enough and Josephine who claimed she did not love me when she really did. Well, thieves and liars would find themselves on the path to damnation unless they ask for forgiveness.

I had desired in times past for the world to pay them in their own coin. Look at what it brought them; endless good things. I must believe that good could come to both an evil man and a good man. In all this, I couldn't tell whether the people I mentioned above felt fulfilled in achieving what they wanted. Was Josephine, who was now married, truly in love? Was Paul truly happy and would he steal no more? That would be left to them to answer. They must have heard of me by now; of my discovered status of a murderer. I expect that they will speak ill of me while forgetting that they too had sinned. It was expected that they speak of me as if I had not been their friend but a vicious being with vicious intentions. I must expect that they must have denied that I was once their friend. After all, if Master was denied by His friends, who was I that I couldn't be denied by my friends? Many will be happy to live in darkness with their secrets until it comes to the light. Then, they shall scramble to hide their shame; to each, his or her own path.

I would seek to work out a path for myself with fear and trembling, for who shall desire to be friends with a killer like me? I must expect to be lonely and without support from people. Despite my evil ways, I must desire to still be good, to do good and to win the heart of men with the little good I had done.

Shall I expect that people will accept me, despite all I had done? Shall I still expect Master to love me, despite what I had done? Would humans be tired of doing good if they see no reward in that? That would be their decision. They had to work out their salvation with fear and trembling as I now did, expecting to be saved.

Ifonelivedindarknessforlong, howcanoneexpecttobelight? One who lives in the dark for long would end up becoming darkness itself. What if one desired to be light, as I did in times past, and yet one couldn't? Shall I say that, in my darkness, I desired for light to prevail and it never came? Could light be so weak as to let darkness reign? It seemed that some are light to the world and others are darkness to the world; that they were both meant to coexist; that both were special. If there was only darkness, we wouldn't appreciate light and If there was only light, we wouldn't appreciate darkness.

I was a fool, as I felt that, if the light I thought was in me led me nowhere, I should have striven to find a way in the darkness rather than run from it. Maybe the light won't save the whole of mankind.

It would take a huge level of courage and determination, of anguish and pain, to pull out of bed each morning in my new house where I hid from the world. In this new place I found for myself, there were new people and living conditions were worse than where I was previously. I had my fortune, which was now was dwindling. It did save me for now and hid me from the world. I struggled to get out of bed each morning, with my past actions tormenting me. I felt that it won't be long before my final days would roll in, bringing me closer to either damnation that I expected or heavenly paradise that I desired.

I failed to value the words said by the mouth of men - creatures I believed I was better than - where I currently find myself. Only a fool would stoop to question those who he knows he is better than. What would he expect to gain from them? What did the creator expect to gain from the created? What shall Master desire to gain from me if He began to answer questions I put to

Him? Nothing! Master will gain nothing, for it was my choice whether I will serve Him or not. Whether I served Master or not does not change Him. If men in the world refused to serve Master, then the stones shall rise and serve Him.

I desired to find meanings in the situation that brought me to this very moment in which I was stuck between the desire to live longer and the anguish of dying. I desired to die, in a bid to rid myself of the pain that came with living, of the disappointments I had experienced and of the shame I had caused to myself and the world. How I brought myself to end a precious life like Aunt Suzzy's was something I couldn't fathom.

Everything about me was about Master and His love that could never fade away. I was a sinner who remains loved by Master. People may live virtuously and yet not live long. Despite my sinful ways, I am still living. Shall we question the creator again? The creator will, in His fury, get tired of endless question asked by the created and seek to return one of them for judgement; to either damnation or heavenly paradise

Could one deeply explain the happenings of the world; a world we could not comprehend, a world where we sometimes receive the opposite of what we desired or wanted? Should we keep trusting in Master if He does not give us what we desired? We will be foolish, if we expect things that don't belong to us. Everything in the world belonged to Master and He gives them to whomever He deems fit.

What shall I say, if I desired to be the best I could and to grow, and these kept eluding me? Should I devise means to be the best and grow, for it was required that I grow in wisdom and in stature? A fool I was, as I left endless question for men - those in light and those in darkness - to answer for themselves.

How can a living man write so accurately about his death? How can one summon the courage to write about his death without feeling severe anguish about whether he is heading to damnation or to heavenly paradise? The end of a person may come so swiftly or unexpected that sometimes, one may lack time to document his or her own history.

If I ever died, despite hiding in the world, some people would be glad to hear that. Could I do anything about that? If death was the destiny of every person, how can one seek to escape the destiny that awaits them; whether in gladness or sadness? On the path to damnation shall humans find themselves, for praying not to die.

My past could be forgiven but my future was one I had given up on; owing to my failure to fully understand the present. I needed to fix the present so I could look at the future with a glimmer of hope, if possible. There was a time to live and a time to die. I desire death but, as always, I'm sure to keep living. Sometimes, people live on when they are expected to die and others die when they are expected to live.

I wanted to be sure of myself, my senses, my thoughts and my actions so far, in the world. I would get terrified of what will become of me and what people would say of me. Well, I should be more terrified if the perceived darkness of damnation was where I was bound to end up. It was something I couldn't bring myself to fully understand. Perhaps, even the light can't fully comprehend the darkness of damnation. On the path of damnation I shall find myself, if I felt that Master's light was something that couldn't comprehend and conquer the darkness of damnation. I was sure that my endless questions and thoughts were likely to kill me.

Having heard countless stories of heavenly paradise and less stories of damnation, I desired the path of redemption and salvation so as to find myself on the path of heavenly paradise. Master had said that He had gone ahead to prepare mansions, for His children, in heavenly paradise. I wanted a mansion as well, but that meant I had to die and rest in peace.

Could I rest in peace if I failed to live in peace within myself, on earth? I endlessly desired that good things will be said of me but what if the world remembers me only for my atrocities? Would that mean I was the worst to have walked the earth? Men will count me among the worst to have walked the world and I shall not blame people for failing to see the little good in me. I must blame myself for hiding myself from the world. I hid the little light I carried, causing it not to shine brightly in the world.

I admonish you to let your light shine.

I felt I had no light now, for I had caused pain to many by killing Aunt Suzzy. This means I had to hide myself from the world so as not to cause further pain to not just myself but also to other beings of the world.

I failed to accept Sophia's love when she offered it. I failed to honour the care and trust of Miriam. When I sought to escape my shell to love Ella, to let my light shine in the world, it led to my downfall. I had opened myself to the workings of the world by desiring to shine my light in it. Maybe if the world comes to know me more than I expected, more than they felt they knew me - not as a murderer that they believed I was - they would come to appreciate and love me the more.

However, this was not the time. I could no longer let the world know more about me. Time was ticking and I could no longer bring out more of my goodness, as the world will only desire to know my evil deeds. Call me a fool for not wanting the world to know about me and for accumulating endless knowledge about the world. In the end, I would be forgotten and so will you, as we will carry our knowledge to the grave.

In all my evil acts, so far, in the world and my desire to find the path of redemption and salvation so as to be saved, I could only find solace in the sweet thoughts of the good I had done in the world. This good included when I: helped the poor, paid the bills of the sick, comforted the afflicted and did many other things I shall not say. With or without my fortune, I had done several good things and repressed them. After all, I shouldn't let the world know that I helped in making it a better place as I followed Master's instructions to not let my left hand know what my right hand was doing; as I did many acts of kindness and goodwill to the world. You must do the same, to make the world a better place.

'What a good son you are!' I believed Mother will say to me if she knew of the good I had done, despite my random evil acts.

What more do you want to hear? What more do you want me to say? I think I'm now void of anything you would call inspiration. It has been sapped from me; leaving me entirely empty. Also, I believe I am void of anything called the end. I think I always found myself at the beginning; the beginning of life and of death. There can't be an end to me as there was no end to Master, for I have become like my Father who is Master.

I spoke of myself like I spoke for the world; you all must forgive me. I already forgave myself and the world. I sought to speak of the world while being of the world.

If these were my thoughts, then they were bound to intertwine with each other. Each may bear a certain resemblance to the other. However, each happened at different times and felt different to me.

I must tell you, this wasn't my story; it was your story. You must now filter through the knowledge you find in here. This is because, in the journey of life, so many things are forgotten, some are learnt and others are 'unlearnt.' You must filter and sieve the knowledge you find in the world, to make sense of it and fully use it to perfection, for the betterment of the world and yourself.

Sometimes, you may be the light and sometimes, you may be the darkness. There's always an end, but again, not an end to me. There's always an end to the light and a beginning of the darkness; as well an an end to the darkness and a beginning of the light. There was a cycle and a pattern to everything and I hoped that I would find myself no longer in darkness but in light.

I must again admonish you, if you are meant for darkness, embrace it and let it become your light. If you find yourself in light, embrace it but occasionally embrace the darkness. By doing so, you become one with the world so as to find yourself wherever it was. Both darkness and light were special and one can not truly exist without the other.

Forgive me again as I cried because I didn't find my purpose. I didn't even know what it was or who I truly was, as I become void of inspiration to go on any longer in this journey with you. I sought to become myself in a bid to understand the world. It was late and I had failed. On the path to eternal damnation I shall find myself, for thinking I was late, as well as for failing to find my true self and my true purpose while I walked the earth. In spite of all this, I did a great job in the world. I was a source of happiness to many and a source of anger as well as pain to some. I could be remembered and I could be forgotten.

Don't forget; there could be no end to me as I desired one whom I loved so much, one I endlessly desired, one whose name is

'Treasure.' 'My treasure,' I would call her. This was not Ella whom I had claimed to love. This was one who I had hidden from my mind and from the world, just like Master did hide many in the world. My treasure would say to me, 'Oh Lifa, how have you been?' with a smile that broke down the stronghold of my life. This could make me come crawling to her or even crying in her bosom.

I knew that Master will be very proud of me, for I had asked for forgiveness and Master will not reject a heart that is broken and sorry for its sins. The host of angels would celebrate a hero that returned home. I shall find myself filled with gladness.

Immediately, I would wake from my imagination - not of my treasure - but from my imaginations of the heavens and the angels welcoming me back to the heavens. I would wake, feeling so heavy, to alluring sounds of silence. It was an illusion; a safe haven that I had created to save myself from the turmoil of living.

I awoke, still buried in my new corner, living and still devising means to conquer a world that had conquered me. I had been given another chance at life; whether by myself or by Master, I couldn't tell. I still desired acceptance from humans. These were the very thoughts I had developed, which I was proud of, as I sought to tackle every evil and bad thought. This was with a desire to save not just myself - for I was already saved - but the world.

I thought of those that played a role in me getting to this very point I found myself: Master who created me, my parents, Aunt

Suzzy who willed me a fortune and to everyone else who played a role; whether knowingly or unknowingly. I also thought of those who would yet play a role, as I found myself still living in the world of men, for we are all connected to each other. I shall be proud of us all and of myself, as my soul desired Master who is the spiritual highest; in hopes that I shall come and appear before Him. I wanted to be sure I was fully deserving of the redemption Master gives rather than of the damnation that I had escaped from.

www.ingramcontent.com/pod-product-compliance
Lightning Source LLC
LaVergne TN
LVHW010543160826
845677LV00013B/2982

* 9 7 8 9 7 8 7 6 6 4 1 2 4 *